crash

Also by **J.A. HENDERSON**

Bunker 10

J.A. Henderson has been described as
'One of the UK's most promising children's writers.'
EDINBURGH EVENING NEWS

PERMISSIONS
The extract about a trawler possibly being sunk by a release of gas in the
North Sea is from the BBC News website **www.bbc.co.uk**

The extract about a tidal wave possibly being triggered by North Sea drilling is repro-
duced by kind permission of the *Evening Chronicle*, Edinburgh, Scotland.

The Ormen Lange extract is from **www.offshore-technology.com**
(the website for the offshore oil and gas industry).

crash

J.A. HENDERSON

OXFORD

UNIVERSITY PRESS

OXFORD

UNIVERSITY PRESS

Great Clarendon Street, Oxford OX2 6DP

Oxford University Press is a department of the University of Oxford.
It furthers the University's objective of excellence in research, scholarship,
and education by publishing worldwide in

Oxford   New York

Auckland   Cape Town   Dar es Salaam   Hong Kong   Karachi
Kuala Lumpur   Madrid   Melbourne   Mexico City   Nairobi
New Delhi   Shanghai   Taipei   Toronto

With offices in

Argentina   Austria   Brazil   Chile   Czech Republic   France   Greece
Guatemala   Hungary   Italy   Japan   Poland   Portugal   Singapore
South Korea   Switzerland   Thailand   Turkey   Ukraine   Vietnam

Oxford is a registered trade mark of Oxford University Press
in the UK and in certain other countries

British Library Cataloguing in Publication Data

Data available

ISBN: 978-0-19-272079-5

1 3 5 7 9 10 8 6 4 2

Printed in Great Britain by Cox and Wyman Ltd, Reading, Berkshire
Paper used in the production of this book is a natural,
recyclable product made from wood grown in sustainable forests.
The manufacturing process conforms to the environmental
regulations of the country of origin.

Thanks to Alison, Catherine, Charlotte, Emily, Jordan, Lucy, Mo, Polly, Sarah, Sean, Siobhan, Veronica and Alex for all their help.

For Charlie
My son

The Norwegian Sea
700 miles nor'-east of the Faroe Islands

The trawler *Lillian Gish* bobbed beside a massive oil derrick, invisible in the cold, dark void below the platform. The number 579 was painted on one gigantic leg of the rig, each number larger than the trawler itself and stained with algae and oily rivulets. The vessel stayed just long enough for three crates to be lowered onto its deck, quickly and quietly, before it chugged off again.

An hour later the craft was ploughing south through choppy waves, thick and mottled as soup, heading back towards the Scottish coast.

The *Lillian Gish* usually carried a crew of seven, but there were only three sailors on this voyage. The fewer people who knew what the trawler was transporting the better.

Eddie Hall peered through the salt-streaked wheelhouse window, holding a tin mug of coffee. Taped to the wooden wheel was a picture of his daughter Elspeth, a solemn five year old sitting alone on a see-saw in Camperdown Park. The photograph was rimmed by oily fingerprints and tape marks—the result of being removed from the young seaman's wallet a thousand times and fastened to the wheel for luck. Elspeth's mother had moved to Aviemore when she and Eddie divorced and he hadn't seen his daughter for two years.

He squinted uneasily out of the grimy window at the heavy sky.

Something wasn't right.

In the six months Eddie had crewed trawlers, he had cultivated a sailor's instinct for trouble, along with a fine walrus moustache. He opened the wheelhouse door and freezing Arctic air cooled the cabin and attacked the condensation on the glass. Steam from his mug swirled back on itself in protest.

There was a strange smell in on the wind. A little like burnt matches, Eddie thought—though that seemed improbable, what with water stretching from horizon to horizon.

The first mate, Lasse Salvesson, was leaning over the stern—tall, pinch-faced, and encased in a full-length black oilskin coat. He would have looked like death itself, were it not for the bright red bobble cap on his head and the industrial sized torch in one hand. He straightened up and glanced over his shoulder.

'Get the skipper up here.'

'At this hour?' Eddie protested. 'I'm not supposed to wake him unless it's an emergency.'

Captain Morrison was a heavy drinker. The alternating pressures of boredom and danger on a fishing boat took its toll on a man, as Eddie now understood. But the captain was the captain and Eddie disapproved of the skipper finding solace in a whisky bottle.

'I don't care if he's in a coma.' Salvesson wiped a trembling hand across his spray-slicked forehead. 'Get him on deck!'

Frightened now, Eddie pulled the brass mouthpiece from the holder on the wall and blew into it. It was connected by a series of tubes to the skipper's cabin and a sharp puff from the wheelhouse produced a piercing whistle at the other end. Eddie took a sly satisfaction in that. He removed the brass cylinder from his mouth and held it to his ear.

'What the hell is it?' Captain Morrison's voice squawked tinnily, as if he were a hundred miles away. He sounded tired and grumpy, but then, he always did. 'We hit an iceberg? We better have.'

'The first mate wants you on the bridge immediately, Skipper,' Eddie replied with false humility. 'Sounds urgent.'

'Tell the bugger I'm going to throw him over the side when I get there.'

A few minutes later Captain Morrison appeared on deck, coatless and hatless, wearing a huge Arran jersey to combat the cold. His thick black hair, streaked with grey, stuck up on his head like a spent firework and his beard was dotted with crumbs. He smelt strongly of alcohol.

'What's going on, Salvesson?' he shouted, ignoring Eddie.

The first mate didn't reply, too busy shining the powerful

torch in arcs across the water. The captain strode to the rail and leaned over.

Eddie saw the skipper's body go rigid. Overcome by curiosity, he locked the wheel and made his way out towards the men. The first mate was shaking his head, his face even paler than normal.

'What the hell *is* this, Captain? Shouldn't we report it to someone?'

'Are you kidding?' Morrison said tersely. 'With what we're carrying?'

'Twenty years I've been a trawlerman,' Salvesson replied stubbornly. 'I never seen such a sight in my life.'

'Neither have I.' The captain scratched his beard. 'But we have to keep quiet about where we are and what we're doing.'

'We should never have taken this job. I said so before we started out.' The first mate crossed himself and spat over the side. 'Our cargo is cursed. I swear it.'

'None of that talk!' Morrison snapped. 'The fishing restrictions in the North Sea have all but destroyed us. We'd no choice but to make this run.' The skipper put a scarred hand on his first mate's shoulder and stamped a foot on the deck. 'Just one trip, Salvesson. We need the money.'

'Yah. *If* we live to collect it.'

'You Norwegians, eh? Always so damned optimistic.' Captain Morrison turned to Eddie as the younger man reached the rail.

'Take a look if you must, boy. Then keep us heading south.' He paused for a second and threw back his shoulders,

4

staggering slightly. 'And maintain radio silence all the way to Scotland.'

Eddie was staring dumbly at the surrounding sea, hands tight on the rails, not feeling the cold seeping into his fingers.

'Understand, sailor?' Captain Morrison repeated.

'Aye, Skipper.' Eddie was still gazing uncomprehendingly over the side. Salvesson played the torch beam across the water, back and forth like a searchlight.

All around the *Lillian Gish*, as far as the eye could see, dead fish layered the ocean. They bumped gently into each other, cresting each swell of the tide, white and bloated as maggots.

The Bridge Over the River Forth

And the second angel poured out his vial upon the sea; and it
became as the blood of a dead man: and every living soul
died in the sea.

REVELATION 16:3

Chapter 1

B obby Berlin lost his father on the 6.15 p.m. train from Edinburgh to Aberdeen.

The day had started off unexpectedly well. Bobby's father, Gordon, had taken the week off work to spend time with his son but was slowly going stir crazy. There was nothing for him to do in Puddledub, the village where they lived, so he had suggested a trip to the cinema in the capital. They had driven to Aberdour and parked the car at the railway station, then taken the express into the city.

'Are we going to see a comedy?' Bobby asked hopefully as they stood in the cinema queue.

'Depends on whether you think a meteor hitting New York is funny.' His father jerked his thumb at a poster showing a skyscraper with a hole in it. Under the picture was a lurid green title. *Fireball!*

Bobby groaned. Now the reason for their trip was clear. Gordon Berlin was a rabid fan of disaster movies, something his son just couldn't appreciate. It wasn't as if any of these films actually ended in *real* catastrophe—some unlikely hero always saved the world in the nick of time.

The attendant looked sceptically at Bobby, who had to stand on his toes to see into the ticket booth.

'This film is a fifteen certificate,' he said. 'The boy looks a bit wee to be fifteen.'

Gordon Berlin glanced down at his fourteen-year-old son and shrugged.

'That's 'cause he smokes.'

The attendant frowned. Bobby, used to his father's warped sense of humour, smiled awkwardly and accepted the tickets.

After the film they ate fish and chips at a nearby café.

'What would we do if *this* country was going to be hit by a meteor?' Bobby was the kind of boy who had questions about everything.

'There'd be a lot of panic, so we'd have to arm ourselves.' His father considered the problem. 'There's a pistol in the attic that belonged to your grandad.'

This was news to Bobby and exciting news at that. It must have showed in his face for his father tapped him sharply on the forehead.

'Don't even *think* of looking for it. It's locked in a drawer.'

'Why did grandad have a gun? Did he get it in the war?'

'I think he got it in a car boot sale. He came home with a parrot once.' Gordon went back to pondering their survival. 'Anyway, we'd take the gun and some tinned food and bottles of water. Then we'd head for the docks and try and get ourselves a boat. Make for some small island.'

'What if the meteor landed in the sea?' his son countered. 'Then there would be a huge tidal wave and all the ships would sink.'

'All the better. Everyone else would be heading inland to get away.' Bobby's father always sounded self-assured, even when he had no idea what he was talking about. 'But it wouldn't be the ship that was important. It would be the lifeboats. We climb into one and fasten the tarpaulin over our heads. Lifeboats are designed to withstand strong impacts and an empty one will float like a cork.'

He seemed to have given the scenario a lot of thought.

'Is that really true?' Bobby didn't like to take anything at face value, especially when it came from his father. Gordon wasn't above inventing facts in order to win an argument.

'Bound to be. Stands to reason.'

'Then wouldn't all the sailors have the same idea?' Bobby took a long gulp of Coke and gave a victorious belch.

'That's why we'd need the gun.' Gordon looked at his watch. 'We better head off or we'll miss the train home.'

Bobby tugged at his arm as they left the café.

'How come we didn't take Angelica with us today?' Angelica was his father's girlfriend.

'Me and Angelica are having a few . . . problems.' Gordon's curt reply signalled that he didn't want to pursue this particular conversation. 'If the earth gets hit by a meteor? We'll take her with us then. OK?'

'It was cool when she went places with us,' Bobby persisted. 'It's like we were a proper family.'

'Yeah.' Gordon Berlin pulled a cigarette from the pocket of his leather jacket and lit it. 'That was one of the problems.'

The village of Puddledub was in the 'kingdom' of Fife in central Scotland. Fife really had been a kingdom once, and some ancient law allowed the little county to keep its grandiose title. To reach it, the train from Edinburgh had to cross the bridge over the River Forth—a mile and a half of gigantic, rust-red, iron diamonds, their tops fading into the darkening winter sky.

Bobby stared out of the window through the criss-crossing girders, watching the lights of North Queensferry on the far shore. He found the sight faintly depressing. There were so many people down there and he would never get the chance to meet most of them. Puddledub only had fifteen houses and his father wasn't exactly the greatest company in the world. He always seemed too preoccupied with his own thoughts.

'This bridge was built in eighteen seventy-nine, a year after the original Tay railway bridge up north.' Gordon derailed Bobby's train of thought. 'The two greatest structures in the world at the time. Then the Tay bridge collapsed during a huge storm. There was a train crossing when it happened and all hundred and seventy-nine passengers were drowned.'

Bobby's eyes shifted down to the grey, wind-blown water. He tried to imagine what he could do to survive if this particular train were plunged into the sluggish abyss.

Not much, he concluded. It worried him that so many situations could suddenly develop over which he would have no control. He couldn't wait to grow up.

Not that being an adult would help much if death came calling in this particular fashion.

'Fifty-seven workers lost their lives constructing *this* bridge.' Gordon Berlin seemed strangely affected by these morbid facts, although Bobby wasn't sure if he was inventing them to make conversation. He wished his father would talk about something more pleasant, or even ask if his son had enjoyed the film.

The sky and the water were darkening to the same colour, bleeding into each other where the Forth widened and became the North Sea. Out in the bay, three oil rigs huddled together, thick legged leviathans awaiting repairs.

Bobby followed the path of a seagull floating up from the choppy waves into the nest of wires and struts.

Suddenly there was the squeal of metal grating on metal and the train gave a violent jerk. The occupants of the carriage lurched forwards, some embedding their faces on the musty seatbacks of the row in front. The train rapidly lost speed and ground to a halt. Nobody seemed hurt, though passengers were muttering indignantly and wiping dust from their faces.

Bobby looked up again and gave a cry.

There was a scaffolder hanging from a small wooden platform fastened to a rivet-studded support seven metres above their carriage. His feet kicked helplessly at empty air and the wind snapped his orange coat back and forth like a flag. Another workman was lying flat on the platform desperately holding onto his companion's arms.

Spotting the developing tragedy, Gordon Berlin grabbed his son by the shoulder and tried to cover his eyes. Then his hand went rigid and slipped away from Bobby's face.

Bobby saw everything.

A sharp gust of wind pulled the dangling man out of his workmate's grasp and he plunged through the struts, arms windmilling, the thin wire of a broken safety harness trailing behind him like a useless tail. Pain and abject horror were plainly visible on the man's face as he plummeted past the window and vanished below the parapet, heading for the freezing, concrete-coloured water.

Bobby turned to his father, desperate for some kind of reassurance. Waiting for him to explain that what they had witnessed was just some wild publicity stunt or a safety training exercise.

But Gordon was staring out of the window with a lost expression. Passengers in the carriage began rising to their feet and pressing themselves against the windows to try and get a better view.

'Is that guy going to be OK, Dad?'

Gordon didn't move.

'Dad?' Bobby grabbed his father by the arm.

Gordon Berlin swallowed hard. Then his eyes rolled up into his head and he slumped sideways onto the seat.

Chapter 2

In Puddledub, Mary Mooney was casting a spell.

Bobby Berlin and Mary Mooney were best friends. As a matter of fact, Bobby was Mary's only friend, since there weren't any other children in the village. Mary lived with her grandmother, was six months older than Bobby, and claimed to be descended from Gypsies. Her grandmother even had an old-fashioned painted caravan in her garden, though Bobby had never seen it actually go anywhere.

Mary sat on the floor of her bedroom with the lights off and the curtains closed. In front of her was a low table draped with a tapestry and topped by three lit candles. On the wooden floor, drawn in chalk, a crude pentagram surrounded her makeshift altar.

Mary went to the landing and checked that her grandmother was still downstairs. The living room door was closed and the teenager could hear the TV blaring in the background. As long as *Coronation Street* was on, it would take an earthquake to tear her gran from the screen.

Mary slunk back and knelt by the low table, sliding an

open book from under the tapestry. She had found it a few days ago, on the top shelf of her gran's bookcase, slipped into the lining of a huge volume of *The History of Poland*. It looked old, and was bound in pleasant smelling leather, with yellowing, hand-written pages.

It was a book of Gypsy incantations.

Mary knew her gran didn't want her to read it—or it wouldn't have been so well concealed. She'd only found it because she was doing a school project on the Second World War and assumed Poland had been involved somehow.

And the old woman would be apoplectic if she knew the spell Mary was attempting.

It was an incantation for talking to the dead.

Mary laid a photograph of her mother and father, still in its wooden frame, face up on the table. Her parents had their arms around each other and were smiling into the camera. Mary's grandmother, Baba Rana, swore that true Gypsies never had their photograph taken. It was an old Romany superstition—travelling folk believed that the soul could separate from the body and be trapped by the camera. Mary's mother and father, of course, had ridiculed this as nonsense.

The teenager laid a magnifying glass on top of the picture. Her parents' faces bulged like cartoon characters, but this was supposed to help with the spell.

She picked up the book and murmured the words on its fragile pages, faltering occasionally as she struggled to make out the spindly handwriting. When she finished, she read the whole thing again, just in case her first attempt had been too hesitant. Mary looked deep into the brown distorted eyes of her mother.

'Are you out there, Mum?' she whispered. 'Would you let me get a tattoo?'

According to the book, you could hear the people in the picture speak if you wished for it hard enough.

Even if they were no longer alive.

Poop poop!

Mary jumped. Twin doors popped open on the cuckoo clock above her bed. A painted yellow bird darted forwards, gave its pathetic little cheep, and jerked back in again before she could find something to throw at it.

'I'm being serious here!' Mary threw up her arms in exasperation. 'Do that again and I'll be waiting with the garden shears. And I know exactly when you're due to come out.'

She turned back to the photograph and tried to concentrate, staring so hard that her eyes started to water.

A breeze ruffled the curtains and the candles flickered. Mary's heart leapt and she scanned the room, searching for some sign that her parents were near. The wind gusted again. Shadows jinked around the walls as the flames bent and spluttered, but the curtains settled back into their uniform façade. The girl held her breath and listened intently.

Nothing.

'What if I just got my nose pierced?'

Still no answer. Sighing, Mary blew out one of the candles and waved the photograph through its smoke—from north to south, and then east to west—ending the spell just as the book instructed. She would try again next week.

The teenager stood up and returned the picture to the cabinet beside the window. At head level was an ornate crucifix—Jesus suspended on a cross, hanging dejectedly on faded wallpaper. He was also a bit squint, which rather detracted from his pained dignity.

'I know Mum and Dad are in Heaven,' she said politely to the effigy. 'So, if they fancied talking to me, surely that would be all right with you?'

The carved features of the Lord were as pained as the faces of her parents were happy—and equally unresponsive.

'I know.' Mary sighed. 'It's probably not allowed. Sorry about the spell, by the way.' She crossed herself and straightened the crucifix. 'But I miss my mum and dad.'

Outside, a dog at the nearby boarding kennels gave a long, drawn out yowl. Mary shuddered. In Gypsy lore a howling dog was a bad sign. She reached for the curtain to see if she could spot the animal but, as she stretched out, an icy gust blew the drapes into her face. The sill housed a collection of fairy figurines and several of them tumbled from their perch and landed on the carpet. Mary staggered back, beating down the curtain, trying not to stand on her precious ornaments. She collided with the top of the bed-side cabinet, lost her balance, and landed flat on her back. A stronger blast of wind swept into the room, lifting the material over her head and, through the open window, she glimpsed a bloated full moon hovering over the black hills of Fife. The candle flames oscillated wildly and the shadow of the drapes pulsed across the ceiling like the beating wings of a giant bat. The next gust of icy air extinguished the beleaguered lights altogether and the room was plunged into darkness.

She heard a crash from the corner of the room.

A second dog began howling. Then a third.

Mary scrabbled across the floor, banging her head on the hard wooden corner of the table. Her outstretched arms connected with the bedroom wall and she scrambled to her feet, feeling with flat palms for the door frame and then the light switch.

'That cuckoo comes out now, I'll have a heart attack!'

She flicked the switch and turned, her back pressed against the wall, a sudden and unreasonable feeling of panic surging through her.

Her bedroom was small with a sloping gabled roof that made it seem even more cramped. A single bed from Ikea, covered with toy trolls, squatted next to the bedside cabinet—both made from cheap, unpainted pine. Her grandmother, trying to brighten the room with a little Romany decorating, had painted the skirting board sunflower yellow and the crooked ceiling sky blue. The cuckoo clock was Baba Rana's idea too, as were the dried clumps of herbs hanging from the ceiling, each wrapped in string and fastened in place with Sellotape. Their pungent aroma mingled with the candle smoke and made Mary feel sick. The bang on her head hadn't helped.

Everything seemed normal.

Except . . .

The crucifix was gone from the wall.

The teenager moved cautiously to the bedside cabinet.

The cross lay in bits on top of her parents' photograph. Jesus had come loose from the base and was in two pieces, face down and arms outstretched as if the plunge had killed him. Below his broken body, shattered glass obscured her mother and father, sparkling like choppy water in the over-head light. The carpet around the cabinet was littered with her fairy figurines, scattered fallen angels embedded in the weave.

Mary crossed herself again.

She was no expert, not like her grandmother, but there was little doubt this was a truly dreadful omen.

'Oh God,' she said, scooping up the broken effigy. 'What have I just done?'

Chapter 3

Nobody noticed Bobby's father collapse. The other passengers were glued to the right-hand windows, or standing on the seats trying to spot the man in the water. Some had taken out mobiles and were talking urgently. One or two were using their phones to take pictures. Others were stunned into silence. The surviving workman was indicating furiously to the train driver. Though the wind whipped his words away, it wasn't hard to guess what he was trying to convey.

Get the train moving! We have to allow rescuers access! The people in these carriages can see what happened!

Weeping, he turned and punched one of the girders so hard that Bobby winced. Chastised, the driver engaged the throttle and the train sluggishly moved off.

Gordon Berlin opened his eyes.

'What happened?' he said weakly.

'You OK, Dad?' Bobby tried to haul his father into a sitting position. Gordon Berlin wasn't a tall man, but he was stocky and muscular and all that Bobby managed to do was pull his father's T-shirt up over his hairy stomach. Gordon shook off his son and levered himself upright, blinking furiously, as if he had just emerged into bright sunlight.

'Hey . . . where am I?' he said, looking around.

'Dad?'

Gordon stared at his son in bewilderment.

'Who the hell are you?'

For a second Bobby thought his father was joking. On the rare occasions when he was in a good mood, Gordon Berlin liked to kid around, telling his son ridiculous stories and pretending they were true. But surely his father would not joke at a time like this.

'It's me, Dad. What's the matter?'

'Stop calling me Dad, you muppet!'

There was something different about Gordon Berlin's voice. He was talking faster than normal, his Scots lilt more thickly pronounced.

'What do you mean?' Bobby inched away from the man. 'Dad? You're scaring me!'

'What're you on about?' Bobby's father spat. 'What's this Dad crap? My name's Dodd Pollen.' He looked around in amazement. 'How did I get on a bloody *train*?'

'No it's not! Your name's Gordon! Gordon Berlin.' Bobby searched his father's face, trying to find some spark of recognition. 'It's me. I'm your son!'

'Don't be stupid!' Gordon pushed the teenager away. His hands stopped, square against Bobby's chest. They were red and thickly veined, with a taint of nicotine on the fingers. He held them up in disbelief.

'What's happened to my hands?'

'Be quiet!' Bobby hissed. 'What's wrong with you?'

'These aren't my hands.' His father's face twisted in disgust. 'These are *old* hands!'

'You're not making sense!'

'What's happened to me? These *can't* be my hands!'

'*Why* not?'

Gordon Berlin clenched his fists and glared at his son.

'Because I'm only fourteen years old!'

Chapter 4

The conductor's voice fizzed over the train intercom, breaking through the hubbub in the carriage.

'Ladies and gentlemen, we're getting reports of some sort of accident on the bridge.'

'Great. We got Einstein punching our tickets.' A fat businessman in a pin-striped suit turned away from the window. He had already accepted that the worker in the water was dead and there was nothing anyone could do about it. The rest of the passengers were talking loudly over each other, trying to come to terms with what had happened.

Bobby's father had fallen silent, feeling his chest and legs as though they were utterly foreign.

'The train will be stopping at Inverkeithing to allow the police on board,' the intercom continued. 'They'd like to question anyone who saw the . . . incident.'

Gordon Berlin's head shot up. He turned to Bobby, eyes bright with fear.

'I don't wanna talk to the police!'

'What's *wrong* with you, Dad?'

'Stop calling me that, you tube! I'll not tell you again.'

Bobby's heart was pounding and his throat felt like sandpaper. The fat man in the suit wandered over.

'You guys OK?'

'Eh . . . yeah. Thanks.' Bobby tried to sound confident. 'My dad . . . eh . . . he's feeling a bit sick. He hit his head when the train stopped.'

Gordon Berlin was a features writer and often claimed that 'the truth only got in the way of a good story'. Living with him, Bobby had picked up how to tell a pretty convincing story when he had to.

'Tell you what,' the businessman said. 'Soon as we get to Inverkeithing, I'm off in the nearest taxi. Once the police realize our carriage was closest to the accident, they'll be questioning us all night.'

'Will they just let you go?'

'I'll say I was asleep the whole journey. Didn't see anything.' The man nodded towards the carriage window. 'Nothing's going to help that poor guy who fell. I got to get up early for work tomorrow.'

'Can we do that too?' Gordon's hands were clasped on his knees in an attempt to hide the fact that they had begun to shake.

'It's your life.' The fat businessman pulled an equally stuffed briefcase from the rack above his head. Bobby noticed that the man's podgy hands were trembling as much as his dad's. He lowered the bag awkwardly onto the seat and some semblance of sympathy finally crept into his voice.

'You should get your old man away too, son. Looks like he might have concussion.'

'Can *we* get a taxi?' Gordon whispered to his son. 'I don't trust the police.'

'We've got our car parked at Aberdour.' Bobby kept his voice low.

'Stop mucking about! I don't know how to drive.'

'All right! All right! We'll get a taxi.' Bobby could see the businessman was trying to listen in to their whispered conversation. He gave the man a wistful smile, tempted to turn over all responsibility to an adult.

But his father, now forlornly examining his stomach, was the person who insisted Bobby should always think before he acted. To try and take control of any situation. The teenager lowered his head, lips pressed together.

'We are now approaching Inverkeithing.' The intercom burst into life again, an automated female voice this time. 'Thank you for travelling with Northern Rail and we hope you enjoyed your trip. Our apologies for any delay.'

'Yeah. Tomorrow it'll be leaves on the line.' The businessman hefted the briefcase under his arm and moved off towards the door.

Gordon Berlin nudged his son.

'Listen, mate. Can you help me out? I don't want to get you into trouble but I need to get away from here.'

'We won't *be* in trouble. The police only want to know what we saw.' Bobby gave one last glance out of the window but the water was flat and unbroken and the sky was growing black. Nobody was swimming for shore.

His father was also looking at the train window. Not through it, but directly *at* it. His reflection, phantom-like, was unmistakable on the dark pane. Gordon touched his face and let out a low moan as his reflection did the same.

'That's not *me*! That's an old man.'

Cold chills raced up Bobby's spine.

'Maybe you're sick or you really did bang your head when the train stopped,' he said. But he was well aware his father hadn't hit his head on anything.

'I don't know. I don't know *what's* going on.' Bobby's father was still transfixed by his visage. 'I know I don't like the police.'

'Why not?'

'I don't remember.' Gordon Berlin moved his head from side to side and the transparent reflection mocked his every move. He turned to Bobby, his eyes as haunted as the ghost in the glass.

'I just got the feeling I done something terrible.'

Chapter 5

Inverkeithing wasn't a large town and the north-bound rail line only had one platform. It was bordered by a tatty white fence and dotted with empty benches, each illuminated by a concrete lamppost. Two policemen waited in the cold as the train pulled up. One got on to talk to passengers and another stood by the exit, blowing into his hands, ready to interview anyone alighting.

Stepping down from the train, Gordon Berlin was visibly afraid.

'You speak to the copper, eh?'

'What?'

'Please!'

'That won't look right.' His son swallowed nervously. 'Just tell them you didn't see anything. And take my hand.'

Together they walked up to the policeman. He smiled sympathetically at them.

'Bad business, eh? On the bridge.'

Bobby's father shuffled his feet. 'We didn't see anything.'

'My dad and I were asleep,' Bobby broke in. 'What happened? Did someone die?'

The policeman looked uncomfortable. Behind them the fat businessman heard Bobby using his excuse and glared at the back of the teenager's head.

'We don't know the exact situation, son.' The policeman looked across at Gordon. 'You were asleep too, sir?'

'Yeah.'

'You live around here? I think I recognize you from somewhere.'

Bobby's father looked blank.

'I bet someone got hit by the train,' Bobby interrupted again. 'I wish I'd seen it. Did you hear anything on your car radio? Was it a suicide? I want to tell my pals at school.'

'We didn't see anything,' Gordon repeated.

'All right, sir.' The policeman stepped back. 'Get the boy home before he goes into overdrive.' He turned to the fat businessman. 'What about you? Don't tell me you were asleep as well . . . '

Bobby and his father moved out of the streetlight and walked quickly towards the taxi rank.

'You got any money?' Gordon whispered. 'I'll pay you back, I promise.'

'You've got the money. Check your pockets.'

Bobby's father rummaged in his leather jacket and pulled out a wad of notes.

'Beezer! There must be thirty quid here!' He smiled at his son for the first time. 'Will it be enough to get me home?'

30

'Of course. Puddledub is only a few miles from Inverkeithing.'

'Puddledub? What kind of a stupid name is that?' His father frowned. '*I* live in Dundee.'

Bobby felt frustration welling inside and tears stung his eyes. Gordon Berlin saw them glisten as they passed under the next streetlight.

'I *don't* live in Dundee, do I?' he said dejectedly.

'No, Dad. And you're not fourteen either. You can see that, can't you?'

'I suppose so.' Gordon studied his hands again.

'Come with me.' Bobby opened the door of the nearest taxi. 'Maybe all you need is a rest. We're going somewhere safe.'

'Where to, gents?' The taxi driver looked like Grounds-keeper Willie from the *Simpsons*. He wore a tatty yellow pullover and smelled of cigarettes.

'Pennywell Cottage in Puddledub, thanks,' Bobby piped up, before his father could mention Dundee again.

'Nae worries.' The taxi pulled out and headed through Inverkeithing. Gordon Berlin leaned over, lips next to his son's ear.

'Thanks, pal.'

Pal? Bobby felt as if his head was going to burst.

'Hey.' The driver turned almost all the way round to address them, even though he was doing fifty miles an hour. 'What happened back there? What are the polis doing at the station?'

'We don't really know,' Bobby answered civilly.

'Eh? I thought you just got off the train. I saw you talking to the copper.'

Gordon Berlin leaned forwards, his face a spider's web of moving shadows. He laid large hands on the back of the driver's seat, the knuckles white. In the darkness his eyes glittered like shattered glass.

'We didn't see *anything*,' he snarled.

And another shiver went up Bobby's spine.

Chapter 6

The Norwegian Sea
300 miles nor'-east of the Orkney Islands

Captain Morrison and Eddie Hall slid the secret cargo across the deck—three wooden packing cases with some language they couldn't read burned into the sides. Lasse Salvesson was due on the next watch, so the captain was letting him sleep.

After prising the boxes open with a crowbar, the skipper went back to the locked wheel and Eddie carefully lifted out bundles wrapped in oilcloth, placed them in empty herring barrels and packed them down with rags. He had no idea what the packages contained, they were different weights and sizes and the thick oilcloth obscured their true shape. Besides, it was a dark night and the trawler's rigging lights could only dent the thick swathes of shadow layering the deck. All the captain had told him was that the cargo was fragile and had to be handled with the utmost care.

'When you're finished, I want you to stick the tops on the barrels and then forget you ever saw them,' the skipper called from the open door of the wheelhouse. 'I'll be glad to do the same, as soon as we've handed them over to our buyer.'

'What's in these crates anyway?'

'They were found by a bunch of workmen in a cave on the coast of Norway.' The skipper expertly evaded the question. 'Secron Oil has a big refinery there. Apparently they were excavating the shore for some new gas pipeline that's getting built.'

'Yeah, but what's *in* them?'

'None of your business. Some bigwig in the oil company claimed them and we're the delivery boys. And yes, it must be highly illegal or there would be no need to hire a fishing trawler to sneak the contents into Scotland.' The skipper wiped his nose with the sleeve of his greatcoat. 'We're being paid handsomely. That's all I need to know.'

After that Eddie worked silently and efficiently. There was little chance of coming across another ship in this deserted stretch of ocean, but his heart was pounding harder than the *Lillian Gish*'s engine. Though part of him thrilled at the idea of being a smuggler, he was mostly afraid and more than a little ashamed.

'That's the last of it, Captain.'

'Dump the empty crates in the sea.' The skipper fastened the wheel and came out on deck. The sky had cleared, the water was perfectly still and they had no trouble pitching the boxes over the side, though Captain Morrison still stumbled once or twice. The smell of whisky surrounded him like overpowering aftershave.

As they turned back from their task Eddie noticed a slim shape twinkling on the deck.

'Wait a minute, Skipper. I think something fell out of one of the oilcloths.'

He bent and picked up the object. A smile split his face.

'It's a tin flute!' he exclaimed. 'I love these things. I had one for years. Could play it pretty well too.'

'Stick it in one of the barrels.' The skipper took the small instrument from the sailor and held it up to the lights. 'Doesn't look very valuable, but it must be worth something or it wouldn't be in with the rest of the stuff.'

Eddie looked crestfallen. Morrison noticed his crewman's disappointed expression.

'You like the sea, Eddie?'

'I suppose.' But there was doubt in the young sailor's voice. 'It's lonely, but I've no choice really. Not many jobs around where I come from.'

'I've no choice either.' The captain tossed the tin whistle from one hand to the other. 'Hard as it is, this life is the only one I know.' He tapped the instrument against one of the barrels. 'But this little lot is worth a fair bit, mister. The money we get for it will let me keep my ship. You take your share and go find a land job, eh? That's your captain's advice.'

'Aye, aye, sir,' Eddie replied despondently.

Captain Morrison looked at the flute in his large calloused hand. He remembered that he used to play one himself, long ago.

'Here. You have this for now.' He held out the instrument. 'But put it straight in the barrel once we reach our destination.'

'Aye, aye, sir!' Eddie snatched the flute before Captain Morrison got over his bout of alcohol-fuelled sentimentality.

'I'm going below,' the skipper grunted. 'Keep an eye on the wheel till Salvesson gets on deck. Try not to steer us into a whale.'

He clumped off unsteadily. Eddie sat down on a mooring bollard, tentatively put the tin whistle to his lips, and began to play. It had been a few years, but the finger positions came back to him as if it was yesterday.

A sweet and lilting sound floated across the deck and over the sea. Eddie took the whistle from his lips and stared at it. The instrument didn't look like much, but it sounded like a classical flute. He put it back in his mouth and began to play again, staring through the rigging at the stars.

'What the hell are you doing?'

Lasse Salvesson stood by the prow, glaring at him. Eddie had been so engrossed, he hadn't seen the first mate come up on deck.

'Where did you get that?' Salvesson pointed a gloved hand at the whistle.

'It came from one of the crates.' The crewman lowered the flute to his knees. 'The skipper said I could keep it till we reach shore.'

'That drunken old fool!' The first mate slammed his hand against the side of the wheelhouse. 'Does he want to invite disaster?'

'What do you mean?'

'The artefacts we are carrying? They are cursed.' The

first mate looked furtively around. 'Tainted by misery and despair and yet you play with one as if it were a toy?'

'I don't understand.' Eddie held the flute behind his back like a guilty child.

'It's not about *understanding*, boy, it's about feeling!' the Norwegian growled. 'Any true man of the sea knows this.'

'I'm sorry.' Despite the apology, Eddie held on to the whistle. 'I just don't see . . . '

'Keep the damned thing. The damage is done.' Lasse Salvesson pulled the black coat tighter around his body. 'Whatever we do, the *Lillian Gish* is doomed.'

Chapter 7

Bobby's father sat on a leather chair in the living room, staring at his many possessions, recognizing none of them. His son perched glumly on the sofa opposite.

'Is that a TV?' Gordon goggled at a huge flat-screen Panasonic taking up half the wall.

'It's *your* TV.'

'Fab! It's bloody huge! Why is there another one on that desk?'

'That's the PC.'

'What's a PC?'

'Can we leave this stuff till later?' Bobby's voice was strained to breaking point. 'I'm feeling a little freaked out.'

'Aye. OK.' Gordon Berlin got up and looked at himself properly in the mirror over the fireplace. The face that stared back had small, even features, countered by large, sleepy green eyes. He looked across at Bobby. The boy's eyes were similar. So were his small nose, thin lips, and square jaw. He turned back to the mirror. The face in the glass really wasn't bad looking.

But it certainly wasn't fourteen.

'All right.' He tugged at his ear and checked one last time that the reflection did the same. 'How old am I really?'

'You're forty-five,' Bobby answered dutifully. 'Your name is Gordon Berlin. You work as a features writer and you're my dad.'

'I'm a journalist!' His father seemed mortified. 'But I was going to work on an oil rig when I was old enough!'

'Well . . . you *did* work for some oil company, but you quit to look after me. So you said, anyway.'

'Really? I don't think I ever intended to have a kid,' Gordon mused. 'Certainly didn't expect him to pop up on a train seat next to me.'

'What *do* you remember? Who do you *think* you are?'

'I don't remember much,' his father admitted. 'My name is Dodd Pollen. I'm fourteen and I live in Dundee. The year is nineteen seventy-seven. Only . . . I bet it's not, is it?'

'No,' Bobby agreed. 'It's two thousand and eight.'

'I suppose I'll have to believe you.' Gordon looked back at the mirror. 'But how did I get old? What *happened* to me?'

'Maybe all you have to do is rest.' Bobby realized that he, for one, was exhausted. 'After a good night's sleep it might all come back to you.'

'Eh? It's only ten o'clock.' Gordon glanced at the clock on the wall. 'What's the point in being an adult if I can't stay up late?'

'You get your memory back and you can stay up for the rest of your life,' Bobby retorted sourly. 'I'll show you where your bedroom is and I'm going to mine.' Bobby headed for the living room door. 'I have to *think*, Dad.'

'All right, all right. But can I read for a while? You got any comics? This week's *Commando*. Or the *2000 AD*?'

'Which makes it a bit out of date.' Bobby shook his head. 'You can have today's *Edinburgh Evening News*. You've got an article at the bottom of page fourteen.'

'Wait a minute!' Gordon Berlin heaved himself out of the chair. 'What did you mean about looking after you? If I'm *really* your dad, then where's my wife? Where's your mother?'

Bobby paused in the doorway and his shoulders tightened.

'She's dead.'

'Oh. Sorry, mate. I mean . . . Bobby,' Gordon said awkwardly. 'Look . . . eh . . . You're right. We'll talk about everything in the morning. I'm a bit confused right now.'

'Join the club.'

'I bet you're right.' The man smiled sheepishly. 'I bet everything will be normal when I wake up. Hey! Maybe I'm dreaming.'

'If you are, it isn't a dream. It's a nightmare.'

Bobby lay staring at the ceiling long into the night, unable to sleep. He tried not to think of his predicament. He tried not to think of his mother. He tried not to think of anything.

But, hour after hour, black feelings tumbled over each other inside his head until he drifted off.

Gordon Berlin's thoughts, however, were far more pleasant. He was utterly mystified, but he could see the advantages of suddenly becoming an adult. He wouldn't have to go to school for a start. He wouldn't get any hassle from parents. He could watch 18 certificate films at the cinema. He hadn't even cleaned his teeth before getting into bed.

And he hadn't taken his nightly pills.

In fact, he had forgotten the pills even existed.

Pills he had never told Bobby about.

Pills that he *had* to take.

[SATURDAY]

Part 2

Dodd Pollen

When I was a child I spake as a child, I understood as a child,
I thought as a child: but when I became a man, I put away
childish things

1 CORINTHIANS 13:11

Chapter 8

The Norwegian Sea
300 miles nor'-east of the Orkney Islands

The crew of the *Amazon* drew alongside three crates bobbing on the murky swells. The trawler had been fishing for mackerel near an area known as Ormen Lange. They were heading back to port in the Shetlands when one of the trawlermen spotted the floating debris.

Captain McRory stood on the prow, hands in his pockets, as the boat cut engines and drifted towards the wooden boxes. One of the crewmen swung a grappling hook, caught the nearest crate and the men hauled it onto the deck. The first mate puffed on a cigarette, shielding it with his hands to stop the sea spray turning it to soggy paper in his mouth.

'You think there's been some sort of accident?' he lisped through the smoke.

'Doubt it.' Captain McRory shook his head. 'There's no oil slick. No wreckage. It's probably jetsam, pitched over the side of another vessel.' He looked at the rising sun. 'Can't have been too long ago, or else they'd have got water-logged and sunk.'

'Why would anyone do that?'

'One of the many mysteries of the sea,' the skipper grinned. 'And none of our concern.'

'I tell you what's a mystery.' One of the older men ran calloused hands over the crate. 'This is made from oak. Nobody makes boxes out of oak any more. And it's got lettering burned into the side. Not stencilled. Burned.' He patted the side of the crate. 'This thing is *old*.'

'Any idea what it says?'

'Not a clue.'

'It's German.' A young crewman named Karston was peering at the letters. 'I used to work in the Rhine ports,' he offered by way of explanation as he knelt beside the crate and studied the writing.

'*Ahnenerbe Forschungs und Lehrgemeinschaft*. It translates as . . . eh . . . *Ancestral Heritage Research and Teaching Society*. And underneath,' the man traced his fingers along the lettering: '*He who ignores the secrets of the past will unleash the power of darkness.*'

'Yeah. Whatever.' Unlike most seamen, Captain McRory wasn't a superstitious man. 'Now, can we get round to the business of transporting our catch?'

'I'll tell the engineer to put us back on course.' The first mate turned towards the wheelhouse. He stopped and sniffed the air.

'You smell that?'

'I certainly do.' Captain McRory frowned. 'Was it you?'

'No, sir!'

The captain slowly took his hands from his pockets. Within a few seconds the acrid smell had become overpowering. The other crewmen were looking at him questioningly. One or two clapped a hand over their mouths, their faces registering revulsion.

'It smells like . . . sulphur,' the first mate said. The stench was now so strong he had difficulty forming the words.

The older crewman crossed himself. 'It's like the very gates of hell have opened.'

Captain McRory fought the impulse to gag.

'Get us moving!' he yelled. 'Full speed ahead!'

The first mate darted into the wheelhouse and the *Amazon*'s engine roared to life. The ship gave a lurch, but it was a downward motion, not forward, as if the craft were in some giant, stuttering lift.

'God save us!' One of his seamen pointed over the side. 'We're sinking!'

'Is the hull breached?' the first mate screamed from the wheelhouse door, losing his balance and falling to one knee. 'It *can't* be!'

Captain McRory had been a sailor for most of his life and he knew the *Amazon* couldn't possibly be letting in water. That would cause the ship to list, not go straight down. He knew *everything* that could cause a trawler this size to sink. A violent storm, a freak wave, even a whirlpool. He raced to the side and stared in disbelief at the water rising rapidly up the side of the *Amazon*.

The sea was perfectly calm.

No ship just goes down like a stone! the captain thought as the waves spilled over the rail. *That's impossible!*

Seconds later, the *Amazon* was heading for the ocean

floor, the crew flailing upwards in a doomed attempt to save their lives.

Only the crates remained, still bobbing gently on the water.

Chapter 9

B obby lay in bed trying not to wake up. The light of
day was poking feebly through the blinds and his
father was moving about downstairs. He couldn't
hear any music, though—and Gordon Berlin always played
music as soon as he got up. Bobby knew the silence was a
bad sign.

The teenager didn't feel as if he'd slept at all. His tangled,
bitter thoughts had turned slowly into black dreams and
then back to dread as he drifted into consciousness. Now he
hid under the covers, exhausted, his mind still filled with
frightening questions.

There was a loud bang somewhere below him. *That* didn't
sound good.

Bobby pulled himself out of bed, showered, and dressed.
Then he sat in his bedroom for a while longer trying to stop
feeling queasy. Finally he went downstairs, a hard ball of dread
lodged somewhere between his heart and his stomach.

Gordon Berlin was slouched on the sofa in a sweatshirt
and underpants, eating toast and drinking a glass of milk.

His hairy legs were splayed wide and he was dishevelled and unshaven. He wasn't even sitting the way he normally did.

'That's a crazy wee oven in the kitchen,' he said. 'If you put a metal dish inside it goes completely mental.'

'It's called a microwave.'

'And I tried to stick the TV on, but it doesn't have any dials. *That's* stupid.'

'You have to use this.' Bobby picked up the remote control and handed it to his father. 'I take it you haven't got your memory back?'

'Nope.' His father took a slurp of milk and gave his son an anxious look. 'Don't I have to go to work or pay bills or something?'

'No. You've got the week off.' Bobby switched on the computer. 'I'll put on some music. You like to listen to music.'

'The little TV plays tunes?'

'The PC? It does everything. Your whole life is on there.'

'Let's have a shufti then!' Gordon regarded the desktop with open curiosity. 'What sort of stuff am I into? I used to like the Rolling Stones and then I heard a new band called the Sex Pistols. They're ace!'

'I don't know half the groups you listen to,' Bobby admitted. 'They're all loud. I know you don't like the Rolling Stones any more. You say they're too old.'

'They're still around? Hey, were they frozen or something? I read that was going to be possible in the future.'

'Dad. You think you're a fourteen year old!' Bobby snapped. 'Why are we talking about the Rolling Stones?'

'I don't have anything else to talk about, do I?' Gordon said petulantly. 'Are Dundee FC still bottom of the First Division?'

'I'm going to get myself some breakfast.' Bobby smoothed down his wet hair and marched into the kitchen.

He made himself coffee and sat at the kitchen table, holding the mug to his chest and glaring morosely at the blackened inside of the microwave. He had to tell someone what was going on, but who? Gordon didn't have any living relatives, as far as he knew, and Angelica was probably mad at him. His mother's family had never liked Gordon Berlin, so they'd be no help. If he told them his father had gone nuts they'd probably have him carted off to the funny farm.

Who could he talk to?

Mary Mooney, he supposed.

She was the only person his age in the village and, though she was pretty annoying, she was weird enough to take something like this in her stride. He'd go and see her after breakfast.

First he'd have to persuade his father to stay in the house and not answer the telephone or go to the door. God knows what would happen if someone came to read the electricity meter. Gordon probably didn't know what electricity was.

He strode back into the living room.

'Dad, I want you to promise me something . . . ' His voice trailed off.

His father was sitting at the PC, staring absorbedly at the screen. Gordon kept all his photographs on the computer and had set that file as a screen saver. The images came up automatically a few minutes after Bobby switched on the machine.

Pictures from his father's past were sliding onto the screen and fading away in a macabre procession of forgotten moments. Gordon Berlin as a young man, with ripped jeans and a purple streak in his hair. Grinning triumphantly in a black cloak at his university graduation. Working at a bar, in an office, as a van driver. Standing on an oil platform wearing a white helmet. Holding court in a pub with a beer in one hand and a cigarette in the other. Travelling across America with a pretty brunette. Arm in arm on a highland mountain with Bobby's mother. Getting married, stiff and awkward in a black suit, his in-laws scowling in the background. Looking proudly down at Bobby, a baby in his arms. Then there was a succession of women in unfamiliar settings. Finally, there was one picture with his teenage son outside the house—both staring glumly at the camera from either side of the doorway.

'Bobby, where are all the other pictures of *you*?' His father didn't turn round. The screen saver cast an eerie luminescence over his hunched silhouette.

The teenager felt a lump in his throat.

'You left when I was a baby. You only came back last year. When my mum . . . ' He couldn't finish the sentence.

His father swivelled round, a tortured expression on his face.

'I just seen my life flash before my eyes. I thought that only happened when people died.'

'Dad. I'm sorry.'

'I don't know who I am, and I don't remember where I've been for the last thirty years.' Gordon Berlin took a shuddering intake of breath. 'I don't even know how to work the TV.'

'Hey, hey! I'll figure out a way to fix this mess.' Bobby moved towards him. To the teenager's astonishment, Gordon Berlin reached out and pulled him close, burying his head in his son's shoulder. His body heaved and he began to cry.

'I'm sorry,' he whispered between sobs. 'I'm acting like a big bloody jessie but I just don't know what to *do*!'

Bobby was too bewildered to react, so he stood with his arms round Gordon's burly chest until the weeping finally subsided.

It was the first time he could remember that his dad had ever held him.

Chapter 10

Mary Mooney was up by eight o'clock, even though it was Saturday. There were so many adventures to pack into a day without school that she couldn't imagine wasting a minute of it. Besides, there was no point lying in. Her grandmother was clattering noisily around the kitchen and the girl could smell bacon and eggs frying. Baba Rana acted as if she was on holiday all the time and Mary could appreciate that. Old people obviously didn't want to fritter away what little time they had left.

Baba Rana wore pink velour tracksuits and chain-smoked. Baba was an old Romany word for 'wise woman' though Mary couldn't see what was so smart about cigarettes. Then again, her gran had an answer for everything.

'Never met a herb that didn't agree with me,' she'd say, lighting another Capstan.

Rana was tucking into breakfast when Mary came downstairs.

'Morning, dearie!' she cackled. 'There's a pot o' coffee on the stove and I made the eggs runny, the way you like 'em.'

'I'm a vegetarian, Gran. Same as always.'

'No harm in askin'.' Baba took a slurp of coffee and a drag of her cigarette. 'In that case, yer toast's in the bread bin, just like the egg was in the hen.'

'Best place I can think of for it.' Mary poured herself coffee and stuck a slice of bread in the toaster.

'Look at this.' Her gran tapped the newspaper on the table. 'There was some kind of train accident on the bridge yesterday evening.'

'Bobby and his dad took a train to Edinburgh and back last night. I wonder if he saw it?' Mary fetched butter from the fridge. 'What did the article say?'

'I only read the headlines, petal. They're the most interesting part.'

'Why don't you put on your glasses?' Mary knew her gran was too long sighted to see the small print. And too proud to admit it.

'What ye doin' today, my sweet?' Baba said hopefully. 'Want to come with me to the post office in Kircaldy? I ordered Sea-Monkeys from a comic.'

'What are Sea-Monkeys, then?'

'Got no idea, honey. The ad says you can grow them in a jar. Who could resist that?'

Mary didn't know any other woman in her seventies who even read comics, never mind ordering the dumb stuff they advertised. Graphic novels filled the shelves of their little living room, along with more weighty tomes about Romany life or the history of European countries.

Then again, Mary didn't know of any woman Baba

Rana's age who would effortlessly walk six miles to Kircaldy and back to pick up a package of Sea-Monkeys, whatever the hell *they* were.

'I . . . eh . . . thought I'd see what Bobby Berlin was up to.' Mary put away the butter and bread, avoiding her gran's disappointed stare by stooping to avoid a particularly long string of sage hanging from the roof. Her own bedroom was bad enough, but the kitchen ceiling looked like a forest canopy. The effect was enhanced in a surreal way, by a large rubber snake curling through the clumps of herbs. There was a joke shop in Kircaldy too.

'You shouldn't go runnin' after that boy all the time,' Rana mumbled through a mouthful of egg. 'He's a handsome young chap but you ignore him for a couple of weeks and he'll do a somersault for a glimpse o' yer knees.'

'That's a picture I can't really imagine. I've got legs like washing poles.'

She glanced disapprovingly at her pale, white thighs shining through the gap in her dressing gown. While Mary was distracted her grandmother pulled a pair of glasses from under the table and stuck them on her veiny nose. They were bright purple, unfeasibly large and had little windscreen wipers on each lens. The teenager lifted her head, the frown on her face deepening.

'You did tell me to put on my glasses,' Rana said innocently. 'And I thought it might rain today.'

Mary's grandmother was always trying to make her laugh, and she usually succeeded. But this morning, the teenager's mood wasn't easily lightened.

'Gran?' she asked tentatively. 'What would happen if you did a spell and got a bad omen?'

'What kind of spell?' Rana was instantly alert. 'Don't you be meddling in things like that, darlin'. If you don't know what you're doing, there's no telling what kind of nasty things you can conjure up.'

Mary cursed herself for being so dumb. Her gran might be old but her mind was sharp as a razor.

'No. I was just asking,' she replied quickly. 'But . . . if you did?'

'I'd thank my lucky stars, dearie.'

'I don't understand. I'm talking about *bad* omens.'

'Me too.' Rana leaned back in her chair. 'A good omen? That's just a ruined surprise. A bad omen is a heads-up from God.'

She took off the glasses and tilted her head at her grand-daughter.

'After all, how are you going to prevent a disaster if you don't know it's coming?'

Chapter 11

Ashley Gosh sat in his leather armchair staring across the landscape, a half empty bottle of wine on the coffee table beside him.

The view was magnificent. His house was perched on top of the Hill of Beath on the Fife coast and looked out, through a massive picture window, over the Forth Estuary towards Edinburgh. The only landmarks that spoiled the view were the chimneys of the Secron Ethylene Plant, puffing imitation clouds into a cobalt blue sky. No matter where he moved the chair they were always visible.

He could hardly complain. He had bought the house specifically because it was near the plant. Now it tortured him to look at it.

He poured another glass of wine. It was pretty early to be drinking but he was a busy man and had to take his pleasure in the few moments he could. Wagner played softly on his expensive sound system. He used to like rock music but these days he favoured something more . . . contemplative?

No. Something more funereal, if he was being honest with himself.

The mobile on the table rang. He ignored it buzzing on the glass table top like some fat annoying fly. A few seconds later, it went off again.

He glanced at the number. It was Maureen, his secretary. Reluctantly he picked up the phone.

'What is it now? I'm not paying you to interrupt me every time you have a bad hair day.'

'I've a message for you.' He could hear his secretary rummaging around on her desk, looking for the appropriate bit of paper. He liked Maureen but she was going to have to go. She just wasn't efficient enough.

'I'll find it in a sec.' The woman sounded flustered. 'Apparently it's a very urgent message.'

'They always are.' Ashley took another sip of his wine. He had been drinking it since the moment he had opened the bottle, even though an aged Burgundy was supposed to be allowed time to breathe.

That would be nice, Ashley Gosh thought. To be allowed time to breathe. He remembered when he bought cheap plonk from the supermarket to drink with his mates. Wine tasted better back then.

'Here we go,' Maureen said with obvious relief. 'There is no communication with rig five seven nine.'

Ashley slammed his glass down so hard on the chair arm that liquid slopped over the rim, splashing red droplets across the Axminster carpet.

'What exactly do you mean by *no* communication?'

'I mean they can't be reached by radio or satellite phone.'

'You *did* say five seven nine?'

'I did.'

'Who else knows?' Gosh's heart began to pound.

'Only the top executives so far. And their secretaries. Oh, and the north-eastern branch who were monitoring communications.'

'I take it there are still nomadic tribes in Outer Mongolia who haven't been alerted.'

'I'm just passing on the message,' his secretary replied in a hurt tone.

'What steps have been taken?'

'There's a chopper on its way to investigate.'

Gosh wound fingers through his blond hair and clenched his fist. Maureen waited patiently.

'Is a video conference being set up?'

'An hour from now. Chopper should have reported back by that time.'

'You keep a lid on this, Maureen. No press. No police. Not yet.'

'I've already been told to keep quiet if I want to have a job tomorrow.' The woman sounded less than pleased by *that* instruction. Ashley didn't bother to inform her that, quite possibly, none of them would have jobs tomorrow.

He struggled out of his armchair and paced up and down, trying to regain his composure.

'Maureen? You still there?'

'Of course.'

'Email me all the data on the Lazarus Project. And I want you to dig up any files we have on a man called Gordon Berlin. Scan them and email them to me as well. And keep quiet about it.'

'I'll look him up.' He could hear his secretary writing down the name. 'Who is he?'

'He's a very clever man with a very big grudge.'

Gosh clicked his phone shut and threw it on the chair. He pulled open the window and let the freezing air dry the sweat that suddenly soaked his face.

Bobby had hit on a way to keep his father out of trouble. Once Gordon had blown his nose and wiped his eyes, his son had shown him how to work the gadgets in the house.

First off had been his father's mobile phone.

'This is absolutely bloody ace,' Gordon enthused, his melancholy fading away as rapidly as it had come. Bobby had to admit that his father, whoever he thought he was, had a much sunnier disposition than before.

Gordon held up the tiny phone in admiration. 'Look at the size of this thing. It's smaller than one of those pocket calculators that just got invented.' His eyes widened. 'Hey! How big are pocket calculators now? They must be the size of, like, a pinhead!'

'They are,' Bobby replied sarcastically. 'But it's OK, because everyone's fingers have got smaller.'

'Really?' His father looked at his hand. 'You having me on?'

Then Bobby demonstrated how to actually work the television remote. That was good for half an hour.

'Fifty channels and still nothing decent to watch,' Gordon complained after a while. 'What the hell are Teletubbies anyway? Are they, like, gnomes or something?' He sounded remarkably like his adult self and Bobby felt a pang of hope. It was quickly crushed.

'I want to go out.' His father turned off the TV with a flourish. 'Are there not any other kids in this horrible wee place?'

'Only Mary Mooney, and you can't exactly hang out with her.'

'How come?'

'Because she really *is* fourteen and you need a shave. It might scare her if you suddenly want to play hide and seek.'

'Hey . . . I'm fourteen, not *ten*.'

'You're forty-five.'

'All right! I'm ancient! So what? I don't feel it, that's the point.'

'This is a little place and everyone knows you. What happens if you bump into Mrs Smith from the boarding kennels?'

'What about it?'

'She fancies you.'

'She does?' Gordon raised an eyebrow.

'She's thirty-eight.'

'Aw! That's disgusting.'

Suddenly Bobby had a brainwave.

'I'll show you how to use the internet! I can surf the internet for hours without getting bored.'

'You can *surf*?'

'You're about to get a gander at real twenty-first century technology.' Bobby led his father to the computer and sat him down. 'This will blow your mind, I promise. You can't look at sexy stuff though,' he added wickedly. 'There's a parental control block on it.'

'That's OK. I'm a parent, aren't I?'

'You'll be a real parent when you remember the access code.' Bobby hit a few buttons and the screen sprang to life.

Chapter 12

Baba Rana had begun walking to Kircaldy. She'd put a parka on top of her pink tracksuit and an old Walkman cassette player was clipped to her waistband. She wished she could afford an iPod, but the only income for herself and her granddaughter came from a meagre pension.

She hadn't been exactly honest with Mary. Baba Rana wasn't going to Kircaldy because she was desperate to get her package of Sea-Monkeys; it was just she had nothing better to do when her granddaughter wasn't around. She couldn't afford a taxi and she couldn't afford to run a car and so she was walking. Besides, she loved the countryside. She always had.

She took the coastal road, for it passed the Secron Ethylene Plant. Somehow Rana was drawn to the place. The plant consisted of a series of boxy processing buildings and neighbouring storage sheds. Towering above that were triple chimneys that burned off the plant's excess gas. At night the flames lit up the sky like enormous candles. During the day the complex looked altogether more sinister, though she wasn't sure why.

The plant was the reason Baba Rana had moved to Puddledub, years ago, though she had never told anyone that fact. But the moment she had seen the sprawling complex, on a day trip to the country, she knew she had to live next to it.

The old woman stuck her hands in her pockets, switched the music off and stared at the chimneys. As always, she was unexpectedly moved and, as usual, she had no idea why.

Tearing her eyes away, she turned to continue her journey.

A small, dark-haired boy popped up from behind the dyke that bordered the road. He looked around fearfully, then clambered over. His clothes were strangely old-fashioned and they certainly weren't warm enough to protect him from the winter chill. He shuffled towards the woman, scanning the deserted road, looking as if he might flee at any moment. The woman took off her headphones and slid them into her pocket.

'Hello, Rana.' The boy gave a timid smile. 'I've been waiting for you.'

Baba Rana frowned at a stranger mentioning her name. He looked to be in his early teens, but there was something about his voice and bearing that made him seem much older.

'Sorry, love,' she said politely. 'Do I know you?'

'I'm not sure.' His wide brown eyes were unblinking. 'But I seem to know *you*.'

'So who are you, young man?' There was something about the boy's voice that sounded vaguely familiar.

'I don't remember. In fact, I'm not certain how I got here.'

'What's your name?'

'Er . . . I don't know that either.' The boy rubbed his eyes. 'I feel like I've been asleep.' He pointed to the chimneys spiking the sky. 'What are those?'

'It's an ethylene plant. It makes gas.'

'I'm sure I've seen it before.'

'What *do* you remember, petal?' Rana was becoming concerned now.

'Not much.' He shrugged. 'The last thing I recall was a train. There was some sort of accident.'

The old woman felt a shudder run through her body. She had just been thinking about the newspaper headline in the paper.

'Well . . . do you know where your parents are?'

'They died a long time ago.' The boy reached out his hand. 'May I walk with you a little?' Rana faltered a second, but he seemed harmless enough and, eventually, she took it. It was small and cold as a dead bird.

They walked together for a few minutes. Rana was overcome by the silliness of her situation, but a part of her was inexplicably excited about this meeting. In a way she felt like a little girl again and it was a fine sensation. The fields were low and level and the cows were painted pearls, grazing in the distance. It was a beautiful landscape.

Then common sense prevailed.

'You really don't know how you got here, sonny? You definitely don't live around these parts.'

'No. I ran away. Away from something terrible.' The boy shut his eyes and concentrated. 'But I think I left behind someone I loved.'

Rana was genuinely concerned now. The boy wasn't making any sense. She wondered if he had concussion. Perhaps he had been in the accident at the bridge and wandered away.

'Maybe we should call the police.'

'No! I have to stay hidden.' The boy gripped Rana's hand tighter.

'Why? Is someone after you?'

'Yes! That's it! That's why I ran away.'

'Now we're getting somewhere.' The old woman leaned over and pulled the boy's collar tighter. 'So, what are you running from?'

'I'm too scared to think about it.' Tears welled up in his wide eyes. 'I know it was something *evil*.'

Rana felt a rash of goosebumps spread across her arms. The boy reached up and softly touched the old woman's cheek. There was a strange smell on his palm, a little like burnt matches, Rana thought.

'We need to inform the authorities about you, darling.'

'No!' Stark terror flashed across the child's face. 'Anything but that!' He backed away, shaking his head. '*You* have to help me, Rana.'

Then he was off, vaulting the stone dyke and heading for the ethylene plant. Baba Rana lifted an arm in protest, then dropped it again. She watched the boy grow smaller until he vanished behind the storage shed.

Her face was freezing where he had touched it, as was the hand he had been holding.

The old woman looked down at her cold wrinkled palm and gave a start.

It was covered in blood.

Chapter 13

Bobby and Gordon sat side by side at the computer, trying to come up with a plan.

'I wish we had Cremola Foam,' his father grunted. 'Raspberry flavour's my fave. And some sweet and sour crisps.'

'I don't think you can buy them any more. They were too full of chemicals.'

'Seems like everything good is gone from this world,' Gordon huffed, sounding just like his old self. This time Bobby wasn't fooled.

'Listen, we can't just hope your memory will come back.' The teenager glanced at a calendar on the wall. 'People are going to start wondering why you're not around.'

'Then we need to figure out why it vanished in the first place,' Gordon said decisively. 'Maybe we should go to Dundee.'

'How's that going to help?'

'The only thing I remember, apart from my name, is that I come from Dundee. We should go there.'

'Yeah, well, it's fifty miles and we'd have to walk, 'cause we only have some grocery money left. Unless you can remember the PIN number for your bank account.'

'My *what* number?'

'Exactly.'

Bobby thought for a minute while Gordon amused himself by making horse noises out of the side of his mouth.

'Tell you what, let's check the internet!' Bobby said. 'We can look up . . . eh . . . what's that word when you can't remember things?'

'Stupid?'

'Amnesia.' Bobby entered the Google search engine, punched in the word and a thousand web listings came up. They contained terms like Korsakoff Syndrome, Anterograde, Retrograde, and Hysterical Amnesia, short-term memory loss, and dissociative disorders.

'Man!' His father gave a whistle. 'There's a lot of forget-ful people in this world.'

'Do you remember how to get *dressed*?'

Gordon glanced down at his skimpy attire.

'What's the point, if I'm not allowed to go out?'

'You want to be sitting in your underpants when Mrs Smith from the boarding kennels comes round to borrow a cup of sugar?'

'I'll get dressed.' Gordon leaped to his feet and rushed upstairs.

When he came down he was wearing the outfit Bobby always associated with his father—a plain black T-shirt, black jeans, and engineer boots. Unlike normal, however, Gordon's thinning hair was gelled up like a hedge.

'Best I could do,' he said dismissively. 'Don't seem to have as much up top as I used to.'

'Fugue State.' Bobby triumphantly tapped the computer screen.

'What's that then? Is it in America?'

'It's a type of memory loss. Found it on the web.' On the desk a printer hummed, churning out pages. Bobby picked up a sheet and read what it said.

'A Fugue State is a type of amnesia characterized by an inability to recall some or all of one's past. This is accompanied by confusion about personal identity, or even the assumption of a new identity. The sufferer often has a desire to travel to some other location, with no clear reason why.'

'Like Dundee?'

'Why else would anyone *want* to go to Dundee?'

'OK, that sounds about right.' Gordon sat down beside his son. Bobby ran a finger down his father's stubbled jaw.

'*Are* you going to shave?'

'Never done it before. Put on some cologne though.'

'I noticed. You could stun an elephant at three hundred yards.'

'That's in case Mrs Smith from the boarding kennels comes round,' Gordon grinned. 'So what do we do to fix this? Hit me on the head with a cricket bat?'

'I'm tempted. But, according to this website, the memory of people in Fugue States usually comes back itself.'

'Cool!' His father slapped the teenager's knee. 'How long does it take?'

'I haven't read it all yet.' Bobby studied the printed pages. 'Here we go. Anything from a matter of hours to . . . eh . . . several years.'

'Ach, it'll be a couple of hours, I bet.' Gordon seemed completely undaunted. 'I already remembered that my boots were kept in the hall cupboard.'

'Dad, you put them there last night.' Bobby got up and fetched his coat.

'Oh . . . yeah. Hey, where are you going?'

'To get the shopping,' the boy said haughtily, pulling up his hood. 'Some of us have responsibilities, you know.'

Chapter 14

Bobby bumped into Mary Mooney on the lane connecting their houses.

'I was just coming over to see you,' she said.

'Wow. Same here. You must be psychic.'

'I am, and you can stop being sarcastic about it.' Mary noticed the dark rings under her friend's eyes. 'What's wrong?'

Bobby frowned. He was a practical boy and Mary's belief in stupid stuff like astrology and the spirit world irritated him. He certainly didn't like it when she guessed things correctly.

'What makes you think something's wrong?'

'You came back in a taxi last night. Where's your dad's car?'

'Chum me to the shop?' Bobby stalled while he tried to think of the best way to start his incredible story. 'I got something to tell you, but . . . I don't know if you're going to believe it.'

'Oh, I probably will.' Mary gave him a bright smile.

Bobby accepted this. He often wondered about Mary's ability to remain unflaggingly cheerful. She was a skinny girl and her lank, blonde hair framed a thin face and eyes that were too deep-set to be attractive. And the Mooneys didn't have much money, so Mary's clothes were always scruffy and out of date. Even her name was plain.

Despite this, the girl retained an unshakeable good humour that Bobby found exasperating. They probably wouldn't be friends if he had anyone else to hang out with, though he'd never admit it to her.

But, right now, Mary's positive attitude was exactly what he needed.

They walked down the silent country lane, lined on either side by dry stone dykes and prickly gorse. In the distance a line of oaks scratched the sky with wintry fingers. After a while Bobby began talking and Mary listened without interruption. They reached the end of the lane and the end of his story at the same time. Bobby went in and bought groceries while Mary sat on the wall outside, swinging her legs and thinking.

He came out carrying a bulging carrier bag and sat beside her.

'So this thing with your dad is really genuine? I mean, straight up?'

'Why would I lie about it?'

'Then I believe you.' Mary didn't mention that her omen from the night before had helped convince her. Bobby would only scoff. She folded her arms and regarded her friend.

'What are you going to do?'

'I have no idea.'

There was a beeping sound in Bobby's pocket. He pulled out his mobile and glanced at the display.

'It's my dad.' He punched *receive* and held the phone to his ear.

Mary could hear Gordon's voice buzzing faintly at the other end. She couldn't make out the words but he sounded animated. Bobby listened, his brow furrowing.

'I'll be right there.' He shut the phone. 'Sorry. I have to go home.'

'What's happened?'

'I left my dad playing with the computer.'

'Let me guess. He tried to feed cheese to the mouse.'

'No. He obviously picks things up fast,' the boy replied tersely.

'He got on to Google and found Dodd Pollen.'

Chapter 15

Bobby discovered his father in the kitchen, head in the fridge.

'God, I need a drink,' the man mumbled from the frosty interior.

'Don't you think it's a bit early?' Bobby retorted before he could stop himself. 'Even for you?'

'What are you talking about? I only want a glass of milk.' There was a loud clinking as his father rummaged around. 'There's nothing in here but bottles of wine and packets of Dairylea Lunchables, whatever they are.'

'You used to be quite . . . eh . . . fond of wine.'

'I did? Should I try some?'

'Absolutely not.' Bobby quickly handed over his groceries. 'I got milk from the shop.'

'Heh, heh. The carton's got spots like a cow.' Gordon shut the fridge door and twisted off the stopper. 'And you can get the milk out without a degree in physics.'

He took a long swig.

'You know, I'm starting to quite like the twenty-first century.'

'Dad!'

'Oh yeah.' Gordon wiped his mouth with the back of his hand. 'You need to check out what I found on this internet thingy. I nearly peed myself when I saw it.'

He trotted through to the computer and scrolled down a page of entries.

'Here. This is an article in the *Dundee Courier*, dated January nineteen seventy-seven.'

Bobby leaned over and read the screen. It wasn't a large article, only a sixteenth of a page, but his jaw dropped when he read it.

Police Give up Search for Missing Boy

Angus police today announced that they had called off the hunt for lost teenager, Gordon 'Dodd' Pollen, who was reported missing five days ago. The fourteen year old left his home in Strathmarten Road in Dundee on the 5th of January after a family argument. According to social workers and teachers, Gordon Pollen was a 'troubled and rebellious boy' who had a history of violence and was often in trouble with the police. Eyewitnesses claim that a youth fitting Pollen's description was spotted crossing Magdalene Green at around 6.30p.m. that night in the direction of Dundee Railway Station. One was certain that the boy was reading a train timetable. The police suspect that, like many runaways, he was intending to take the express to London.

'Below the article was a small photograph of a sullen teenager with a sharp face and brown wavy hair.

'That's it. That's all I could find.'

Bobby studied the photograph.

'*Is* that you?'

Bobby's father turned to face him. 'Dunno. What do you think?'

Gordon Berlin had a bull neck and thinning hair, but his lips were thin like the boy in the picture and the eyes looked vaguely similar.

'I can't tell.' Bobby squinted at the image. 'The photo's thirty years old and blurry. I suppose it *could* be you, but that doesn't make sense.'

A thought suddenly occurred to him. 'You've got a whole file of photographs scanned on to the computer. Why don't we compare them?'

'I tried, but there's no pictures of me as a kid.' Gordon opened his photograph folder with a few taps on the keys.

'You're picking up this computer stuff fast.'

'I'm a natural at modern technology. You should see me fix a Chopper bike.' His father enlarged one of the pictures. 'This one looks like the earliest photo, but I must be in my twenties.'

The screen showed a surly young man wearing a biker jacket and leaning against a wall.

'Can't believe I had a purple streak in my hair. I was pretty cool, eh?'

'If you say so.' Bobby could see a vague similarity

between the man in the picture and the newspaper photo-graph, but was far from sure they were the same person.

'This is dumb. You can't really be someone called Dodd Pollen. I bet you've got a passport and everything.'

'Well, I must have a mum and dad.' Bobby's father clicked the file closed. 'Why don't we just ask them?'

'Your parents? They *did* live in Dundee, but they've been dead for—' Bobby stopped in mid-sentence. 'Sorry. You . . . wouldn't remember.'

Gordon seemed more put out than upset.

'Is there anybody in my bloody family left alive?' he snorted. 'Apart from you, that is.'

'No, there isn't.' Bobby's eyes welled up at his father's insensitivity. 'I wish there were.'

'Sorry, pal.' Gordon looked ashamed. 'I mean, sorry, son. I suppose forgetting is a good thing sometimes.'

'You never talked to Gran and Grandad Berlin much anyway.'

'Yeah, well I doubt they adopted a teenage runaway and changed his name without anyone getting suspicious. Anyhow the police seemed to think this Dodd Pollen was heading away from Dundee. Getting a train to London.'

'Maybe you changed your mind.'

'Maybe I'm not Dodd Pollen.' His father sounded doubt-ful but Bobby mentally crossed his fingers. *He* certainly hoped not. But he had more pressing concerns right now. He bit his lip and took the plunge.

'Dad, I think it's time we called the police. We can't work this out ourselves.'

'No,' his father replied quickly. 'I got issues with authority. That's one thing I *am* sure of, even if I don't know why.'

'You might be ill,' Bobby persisted. 'You might get worse.'

'No way.' Gordon jutted out his jaw, as he always did when his mind was made up. But his son couldn't let it go.

'You might need a doctor or something.'

'Just leave it, Bobby. We can do this ourselves.'

'What if we called some of your friends?' Bobby held up his father's mobile. 'Their numbers must be on here!'

'Just give me time to think, will you!'

'Look. Here's Doctor Lambert's number. I could call him and ask . . . '

'I said NO!' Gordon slammed a beefy hand on the computer desk. The glass of milk leapt into the air in an arc of white as he spun round, his clenched fist inches from his son's face. Bobby shrank away, his mouth open.

His father's whole demeanour seemed to have changed. His shoulders were hunched almost up to his ears and his thick neck was flushed an angry hue. He grabbed the boy by the neck and leaned in close.

'I will *NOT* go back!'

Bobby tore himself away, clutching at his throat.

'Sorry! I'm sorry!' Gordon threw up his hands in horror. Bobby retreated a few paces, eyes wide.

'No, really! I'm sorry, pal! Don't know what happened there! I guess I'm feeling a bit . . . eh . . . tense.' Gordon turned back to the computer, as if ignoring the outburst would make everything all right. 'Look. Just let it go. OK?'

'OK, Dad,' Bobby murmured, his heart thundering.

But a part of the newspaper article he had just read flashed into his mind.

Dodd Pollen was a troubled and rebellious boy who had a history of violence.

Chapter 16

A dozen men and women were gathered round the rectangular boardroom table in company head-quarters. Tiny cameras in the roof pointed accusingly at the apprehensive group. Several other faces filled the screens of slim monitors on the wall.

There was no small talk. Every expression was bleak.

'We've gathered all the board members we can reach.' A tall, grey-haired man in a razor-sharp black suit sat at the head of the table, hands clasped in front of him. 'We haven't time to chase the rest down.'

'What seems to be the problem?' On one of the screens an overweight woman in a lavender top lit a cigarette and was obscured for a few seconds by a grey haze.

'There has been no communication with drilling platform five seven nine in the Norway Sea for four hours, Madam Chairwoman, so we sent a helicopter to investigate.'

'And?'

'The platform is no longer there.'

'Oh?' Surprise flashed across the woman's face, but she

recovered her composure quickly. 'Where exactly has it gone?'

'That's the problem.' The man with the grey hair scratched his lip. 'It's a floating rig but it's securely moored. It can't have gone anywhere.'

'That's obviously debatable.' The woman gave him a withering look. 'Since it's not where it's supposed to be.'

'OK. Even if it drifted, it's a hundred and seventy metres across and weighs thousands of tonnes. It could only have moved a short distance and the chopper would have spotted it.'

'And the rig would have radioed their position if the moorings broke,' another executive broke in.

'Are you telling me it sank?' The chairwoman turned on him.

'It's unsinkable, ma'am.'

'That's what they said about the *Titanic*.' The woman took another drag on her cigarette. 'Were there adverse weather conditions?'

'There isn't a hint of a storm. Been that way for hours. But we are getting unconfirmed reports of other craft vanishing in the North Sea.'

'My God.' A young man with a thick black fringe tugged at his tie. 'We've got our very own Bermuda Triangle.'

'Less of that,' the chairwoman snapped. 'Are we talking sabotage? Industrial espionage?'

There was an awkward silence.

'We don't have an explanation,' the man with the fringe said softly.

Ashley Gosh spoke from the screen above the chair-woman's head.

'Rig five seven nine is where Gordon Berlin was stationed. He was working on the Lazarus Project.'

The board members looked at each other. On the screens, four or five faces paled.

'I'm aware of that.' The chairwoman leaned back in her seat. 'Just didn't want to think about it.'

'What will we do?'

'If the platform doesn't miraculously turn up, we'll have to play the hand we're dealt. Mr Gosh, you were head of the Lazarus Project, so you will be in charge of contacting and liaising with the appropriate authorities. *If* it comes to that.'

'I . . . eh . . . '

' "Yes, ma'am" is the correct response.' The chairwoman looked heartily sorry that she couldn't reach out of the screen and grab Gosh by the throat. 'And you'd better be prepared to do some fast talking.'

'Ma'am.' The man with the grey hair put his head in his hands. 'If the Lazarus Project has gone wrong, we're doomed.'

'Then I hope you all have contingency plans.'

'What about Gordon Berlin?'

'Mr Gosh will make sure that every piece of information about that man is destroyed before he contacts the author-ities. I'll see to the rest.' The chairwoman angrily stubbed out her cigarette.

'As far as you're all concerned, Mr Berlin no longer exists.'

* * *

'That vehicle's been here all night.' Constable MacDonald indicated the black BMW at the end of Aberdour railway station car park, next to a sign that read NO OVERNIGHT PARKING. 'Maybe it's a terrorist bomb. Going to blow up our famous flowerbed display.'

WPC Arnold gave a half-hearted smile. She was the only policewoman in the Aberdour area, and MacDonald had the Inverkeithing beat down the road, so they often patrolled together. But WPC Arnold had never got used to her companion's weird sense of humour and, besides, she recognized the BMW.

'The car belongs to a guy called Gordon Berlin. He lives over in Puddledub.'

'A pal of yours?'

WPC Arnold considered that.

'Not really. He doesn't seem to have any friends. We've drunk in the pub together a few times.' She didn't add that Gordon Berlin had flirted with her outrageously each time they did.

'Wait a minute. Does he have a son? A teenager?'

'Bobby? Aye. That's him. Gordon Berlin writes for the Edinburgh papers, so he probably stayed there last night.'

'No, he didn't.' The constable tapped his nose. 'He got off the train at Inverkeithing. I *thought* I recognized him.'

'So?' WPC Arnold shrugged. 'Maybe the vehicle broke down on the way out and he decided to get a taxi back. It's easier to do that at Inverkeithing.'

'Cars usually break down in awkward places.' Constable MacDonald peered through the window of the BMW, shielding his eyes with his hand. 'Awful convenient to grind to a halt in a car park, eh?'

'Maybe he'd been drinking and didn't want to drive. He likes to drink.'

'I would have smelled it. Besides, he had the kid with him.' The constable jiggled the car's handle. 'We were investigating a suspicious death on the Forth Bridge last night, you know.'

'I do.' WPC Arnold sighed. 'You've told me four times already. And it was an accident. Not a suspicious death.' She pulled a mobile from her pocket. 'Tell you what. I'll give him a call, all right?'

'You got his number on your mobile?'

'He gave it to me.' WPC Arnold gave a smug grin. 'He's quite cute, as a matter of fact.'

She pressed dial and held the phone to her ear.

'Hello. Oh. Is that Bobby? Hi, Bobby. This is WPC Arnold over in Aberdour. Is your father there? No. Do you know when he'll be back? You don't.' Arnold repeated Bobby's answers so that MacDonald could follow the conversation. 'Do you know where he is? You don't. No, that's all right. No. No. It's nothing. Just wondering when he was going to pick up his car. It's been in the station car park all night. You didn't know . . . Well, thanks anyway. I'll give him a bell later.'

'Boy doesn't know much, does he?'

'He sounded a bit strange,' WPC Arnold agreed. 'Like he was flustered. Or scared.'

'Or lying.'

'Not that I want to buy into your warped view of the world, but . . . yes.' She snapped the phone shut and put it away.

'It's the flowerbeds, I tell you.'

'All right, Sherlock. Let's finish our rounds. If we don't come across a plot to wipe Aberdour off the map we'll pay a wee visit to Gordon Berlin's house.'

Chapter 17

B obby sat trembling on the couch, wondering what to do. He couldn't tell his father about the telephone call from the police. He was too afraid of how Gordon would react. Bobby could hear his father in the study, playing on the X-Box, whooping with delight every time he killed a bad guy.

The teenager was angry and confused. His life had gone rapidly downhill over the last couple of years. He had loved living in the country and loved his mother and the two of them hadn't needed anyone but each other. Then she died.

Gordon Berlin had turned up at the funeral. An edgy, handsome man in black leather, he had stood at the back of the church with his hands in his pockets, showing little emotion. Bobby hadn't even known who the stranger was until his mother's relatives reluctantly pointed him out.

He had gone to talk to his father, despite their objections.

'I figured you and your mum were better off without me,' Gordon Berlin said simply. 'I know that's not much of an excuse.'

'We were. And it's not.' Bobby was surprised by his own boldness. But his father had nodded in accord.

'It's going to get very lonely for you now.' Gordon ignored the black looks from his ex-wife's family. 'It's probably too late, I know, but I'd like to make amends. If you'll accept my help.'

'I'll be fine.'

Gordon glanced across at the disapproving group.

'Your mother wasn't like the rest of her family. They'll probably send you to some boarding school where you learn to walk with books balanced on your head.'

'And what about you?'

'Let's just say I'm older and wiser. I'm a poor substitute for your mum, but it's better than nothing. I have a great pad in Glasgow with a forty-two inch screen plasma TV.'

'I want to live in Puddledub.'

His father hesitated.

'All right,' he said finally. 'We can live in Puddledub if you like.'

He bent down so that his lips were next to his son's ear.

'I just want to protect you.'

'Protect me?' The boy didn't understand. 'What do you mean? I don't even *know* you.'

'Then now's your best chance,' his father replied evenly.

A week later Gordon had moved into Pennywell Cottage.

But Bobby hadn't become less lonely. His father could be charming and amusing, but he drank like a fish and was prone to black moods that lasted for days. He obviously hated living in the middle of nowhere and found solace in alcohol and a string of women who were neither as funny nor as clever as Bobby's mum. Even when he spent time with his son, Gordon's mind seemed to be on other things, as if he had an inner melancholy no amount of joking could cover up.

Bobby had hoped that, somehow, this would change and a real bond would develop between them. That they'd go kite flying or something, and his father would lighten up and actually enjoy being with his son.

It hadn't happened.

Bobby hated to admit it, but he felt his father was looking after him out of some belated sense of duty, rather than love.

On the other hand, this Dodd Pollen character was light-hearted and easy going, despite his predicament. More than that, Dodd liked and needed him.

But Bobby Berlin didn't want a forty-five-year-old pal. He wanted a real dad.

Besides, no matter how grumpy or depressed his father had been, Gordon Berlin had never raised a hand to his son.

Dodd Pollen had.

Chapter 18

Baba Rana pushed the chair in her bedroom up against the wardrobe. She leaned a hand carefully against the back and climbed on to the seat, lit cigarette dangling from her lips. Her hips clicked noisily, the chair wobbled, and she gave a little squeak of fear, slamming both palms against the wardrobe door.

'Be *very* careful not to fall, Rana,' she gasped. 'You don't want Mary finding you dead on your back with both legs sticking up in the air. That's just not dignified.'

She lifted a suitcase off the top of the wardrobe and dropped it on the floor. A cloud of dust rose from the battered surface as it landed.

Rana slowly got down, knelt beside the case and opened the lid. Inside were the few knick-knacks she had kept from her younger days. She hadn't looked at them for years but the strange boy had started a niggling feeling in the back of her head and Baba Rana *never* ignored her feelings.

She lifted out half-forgotten possessions. There was a silver hip flask that belonged to her husband, long dead now, and a faded picture of them both. They were arm in arm, grinning at the camera.

We both looked so young, she thought, regretfully.

'I hope to see you again soon, Pieter.' She gave the picture a gentle kiss. 'And you better have got rid of that moustache. You know I never liked it.'

Most of the objects in the case dated from her marriage to Pieter, whom she had met in a grocer's shop in Amsterdam when she was seventeen. It was he who had moved them to Britain in search of a better life.

She had virtually no memories before meeting her husband and even fewer possessions. Rana had grown up in an institution—one of the thousands of children orphaned by the Second World War. If she was honest, it was a time she was glad to have forgotten.

She burrowed to the bottom of the suitcase and found the two things she had salvaged from her childhood. One was an embroidered red ribbon studded with glass beads. Rana didn't know where she had got it or even why she kept it. On impulse, she pulled it out and threw it on the bed.

Underneath was an old sketchbook, covered in cracked leather. She had loved to draw as a child and had kept the tattered volume under her mattress at the orphanage. Rana opened up the book and flicked through the pages.

There were pencil drawings of other children, the view from the orphanage window, and a few sketches of gypsy caravans that must have been drawn from memory. Memories she could no longer recall.

And then there were sketches of the Secron Ethylene Plant. Pictures she had put on paper thirty years before the structure had even been built.

Baba Rana shook her head in wonderment, just as she had done the first time she saw the plant. The woman had known, from the moment she set eyes on it, that she *had* to live in Puddledub. She still didn't understand why—or how she could have drawn something in another country that didn't exist at the time.

Now she had a clue.

Rana flicked through the pages until she found the picture she was looking for. When she came to it she gave a shudder. It was dated *5th May 1950*. Again, it was a remarkable likeness of the ethylene plant—Baba Rana had been a talented artist.

In front of the buildings she had drawn a boy. He was small and serious and there was no mistaking his face.

It was the child she had met that morning.

Chapter 19

Bobby badly wanted to share his knowledge of the newspaper article with someone adult, but Mary was the only person he could really trust. Unfortunately, she didn't have a mobile phone—claiming there was no point as she never had enough money for credit. Sighing, he pulled out his own mobile and dialled the number for Mary's house, praying that Baba Rana wouldn't pick up. She was a sweet old lady, but she was even crazier than her granddaughter.

The phone rang several times before a quavering voice answered. He groaned inwardly.

'Is that young Bobby?' Baba Rana quivered. 'I so rarely get gentleman callers.'

'I was wondering if Mary was around?'

'I sent her on a few errands, dearie. She went to the shop to pay for the week's papers. After that, I think she's going to church.'

'It's Saturday afternoon. Won't it be shut?'

'You don't worship much, do you, sonny?' He heard a

sharp intake of breath as Baba Rana took an enormous drag on her cigarette. 'But you're very welcome to come over and wait. Ever seen a real Sea-Monkey? I been watching mine for hours but they don't seem to do anything.'

'I'd love to . . . ' the boy began.

'You would?'

'But I think I'll go and find her. Sorry.'

'That's all right, lad.' Baba Rana tried to keep the disappointment out of her voice. 'Today's ironing day. I've got a lot of wrinkles need sorting.'

'That's an image I didn't need in my head right now.' Bobby wrinkled his nose, holding a hand over the mouthpiece.

'Bobby?' Baba Rana's voice broke in. 'You haven't . . . eh . . . noticed a strange new boy in the village, have you? A boy about your own age?'

'No I haven't,' Bobby said quickly. 'Why do you ask?'

'No reason, son,' Baba Rana replied in a quiet voice. 'Just an old woman being paranoid . . . '

Then she hung up.

Chapter 20

'Where are you going?' Gordon appeared in the hallway as his son was pulling on a coat.

'I'm going to the newsagent's and then the church on the other side of the hill.'

'Don't you dare tell me we're religious.'

'No. I'm looking for Mary Mooney.'

'Good. I can't stand churches.' His father gave a disapproving sneer. 'Bunch of bloody hypocrites work in them.'

Bobby stopped in the doorway. 'What makes you say that?'

'I've forgotten who I am.' Gordon tapped his head. 'Doesn't mean I'm stupid.'

'What? Do you remember something?'

'Some things I just know.' His father gave a throaty cough and padded back into the living room scratching his chest. 'I know I hate religion.'

'Jeez. I hope the Jehovah's Witnesses don't come to the door while I'm gone.' Bobby pulled up his zip and let himself out.

He checked at the local shop but Mary had been and gone, so he set off down the road towards the Catholic church on the other side of the hill. Our Lady of the Sacred Heart was a small Victorian building a mile from Puddledub and a few hundred yards from the far more imposing ethylene plant. The church was surrounded by a low stone wall topped with a carefully tended hedge.

Bobby had never been inside and hadn't realized that the Sacred Heart was usually left unlocked. It stood to reason, now that he thought about it. There wasn't exactly a lot of crime in the isolated villages around Puddledub.

He pushed open the arched wooden door and let himself into the building.

Winter sunlight filtered through stained-glass windows and motes of dust danced in the beams that drifted from the arched ceiling towards the marbled floor. On the far wall above the altar, Jesus hung on a giant wooden crucifix, closed eyes oblivious to the empty mahogany pews.

Mary was kneeling in the front row with her back to him and her head bowed. She was lost in a world of worship and Bobby envied the comfort she found in faith. He didn't understand how Mary managed to find solace in just about everything.

Bobby's mother had believed in God. Now she was gone.

His father, on the other hand, hadn't believed in anything, not even himself. And he was much more persuasive.

'God to Joan of Puddledub!' Bobby hissed in a stage whisper. 'You're getting your knees dirty.'

Mary whirled round.

'Bobby!' She clutched at her chest. 'You can't say that in here.'

'I guess I've got issues with authority.' Bobby sauntered down the aisle in a display of bravado, his hands jammed in his pockets. 'Anyway, I thought you worshipped fairies and magic and stuff.' He nodded up to the cross. 'What's that got to do with the big guy?'

'I like to keep an open mind.' Mary ignored the jibe. 'You could always pray for your dad, since you're here.'

'I doubt he'd appreciate it. He just went on a big tear about religion, though, of course, he can't remember why.'

'There has to be a reason.' Mary was suddenly curious.

But Bobby didn't hear. He was turning on the spot, admiring the majestic furnishings and intricate carvings. He stopped and pointed to a row of wooden cubicles with ornately fashioned doors.

'What are those?'

'You've never been in a confession booth?'

'I'm not Catholic. I'm not even religious.'

'You go into the booth and you can tell the priest anything.' The girl got up and led Bobby to the nearest cubicle. It contained a simple backless seat covered in red velvet and a small window that looked like a serving hatch. 'It's totally private. Whoever you confess to isn't allowed to say anything to anybody and they have to try and help you.'

'Aye. And then everything is magically OK?' The boy stuck his head inside and sniffed. The smell of polish covered a faint odour of sweat.

'No. But it makes you feel better.' Mary gave Bobby a

little shove. 'Go on. You get in the next one and I'll go in here. If you like, I'll start and you can hear my confession.'

She looked around the church to make sure it was empty, and then darted into the booth and shut the door. Seconds later the hatch to the adjoining box slid open and she could see the outline of a figure through the mesh. Mary clasped her hands on her knees.

Suddenly she was acutely aware that she couldn't lie. Not in a confession booth. For a fleeting second she considered telling Bobby how she really felt about him, but she didn't know how to phrase the words. Ashamed at her lack of courage, she decided to trust him with her other great secret.

'Here's a confession,' she whispered. 'My grandmother isn't what she seems to be and neither am I . . . ' She hesitated, unsure of how to continue.

There was a deep breath from the other side of the hatch.

'And neither is Dodd Pollen, Mary.'

The voice coming through the mesh was deep, throaty, and utterly menacing. And it didn't belong to Bobby.

The girl gave a small moan of fear.

'Dodd Pollen is here to stay,' the voice rasped. 'And God help any do-gooders who try and change that.'

Mary jerked backwards, slamming into the wall so hard that the whole structure shook. The cubicle door swung open and her mouth opened in silent terror.

'Mary?' Bobby's head poked through the doorway. 'I can't get into the other box. It must be locked.'

The girl leaped to her feet, pushing him back into the church.

'Run!'

'Why? What are you . . . ?' Bobby began, but one look at his friend's terrified face silenced him. He glanced at the adjoining booth. 'Is the *priest* in there?'

'Just *run*!'

Mary hauled on his arm and pulled him up the aisle and out of the building.

Chapter 21

'What just *happened* back there?'

Bobby and Mary had sprinted across three white-coated fields, blasts of condensed air bursting from their mouths, until they found an adequate place to hide. Now they sat behind a low wall, letting their breathing get back to normal. Mary was shaking all over.

'There was something in the other confession booth.'

'It must have been the priest.' Bobby leaned his head against the mossy dyke. 'He won't have seen us though. We could've won an Olympic gold in cross country just then.'

Mary kept her eyes down, staring at the rutted tractor tracks running parallel to the dyke. She didn't know *what* to tell her friend.

'Your dad found out something about Dodd Pollen on the internet,' she said. 'What was it?'

'Not much.' The boy fished a pair of black woollen gloves from his pocket and pulled them on. 'Turns out he was a real kid who vanished in Dundee about thirty years ago.'

'Did he die?'

'I hope so.' Bobby tried to zip up his coat, the gloved fingers making the simple manoeuvre a laborious task. 'I don't want to sound rotten but it would prove that Dodd Pollen and my dad are different people.'

'Maybe there's another explanation.'

'What do you mean?' Bobby finally managed to pull up his zip. 'And don't be giving me any of your mumbo jumbo hoodoo voodoo.'

'Ssssh.' Mary held up her hand. 'You hear something?'

The boy cocked his head. 'I can hear barking.'

'It's the dogs at Smith's kennel. They sound like they're going nuts.' Mary shuddered. 'Why are they acting like that?'

'They're probably being attacked by a polar bear.'

'Pardon?'

'After the last couple of days, nothing could surprise me.' Bobby vaulted the wall and headed in the direction of the barking. 'C'mon. Let's check it out.'

Mary thought about the sinister voice in the church.

'I don't think your surprises are over,' she muttered, following Bobby over the dyke.

Smith's Boarding Kennel had its own little road leading to the main gate but the barking was coming from the left. The compound was filled with wooden sheds for the animals and a high wire fence surrounded the entire property, allowing the dogs to roam freely during the day. Following the fence, the children pushed through moisture laden branches, heading in the direction of the noise.

'I wonder where Mrs Smith is.' Bobby held a bough back to let Mary get past. 'She normally runs this place like some doggie concentration camp.'

Then the trees ended and they found themselves in a small clearing.

There were five dogs on the other side of the fence. A couple of Alsatians, a Dobermann, and two mongrels, all barking, slavering, and throwing themselves against the barrier, desperate to get at the person standing on the other side.

It was Bobby's father.

'Dad! What are you doing here?'

Gordon Berlin's head jerked round, his eyes wide. Then he spotted who had shouted and a nervous grin sprouted on his face.

'I thought I'd do a bit of exploring. What are these, eh? Killer guard dogs or something? Good job this bloody fence is here or I'd have been torn to bits.'

'They're people's pets.' Mary edged away from the slavering hounds. 'I've never seen them act like this.'

'You must be Mary.' Gordon Berlin gave a friendly wave. 'I'm Dodd Poll—eh, I'm Bobby's dad.' He gave his son a quick thumbs up.

'She knows who you are, Dad.'

'Yes, of course. Bobby's . . . eh . . . a fine young lad and I like him very much.' Gordon pulled himself erect and tried to look manly—though the effect was spoiled by his gelled-up punk hairstyle. 'Yes. And I hope you're attending to your studies at school and all that.'

'I mean she knows about Dodd Pollen.'

'Ah, good.' Gordon nodded towards the frenzy. 'You think we could carry on this conversation somewhere else? These pooches don't seem to like me.'

'Yeah. Let's get out of here.' Bobby pushed his father away from the fence and into the trees. He glanced back once at the snarling dogs.

'I don't know what's possessed them.'

'They always liked your dad before.' Mary glanced suspiciously at the retreating Berlins. 'I'm not sure it's the *dogs* that are possessed.'

Chapter 22

'So what team do you support?' Gordon plodded along beside Mary, trying to make conversation. 'I used to support Dundee FC, before Davie White took over as the manager—then they were rubbish.'

'I don't really follow football,' the girl said shyly.

'Ach, me neither. What about bands? I really liked the Rolling Stones but then I heard a new band called the Sex Pistols. They're ace.'

'Dad!'

'Yeah, sorry.' Bobby's father smoothed down his gelled hair with a guilty smile. 'I write articles for a newspaper, you know. I've got a degree.'

The girl shot Bobby a look of thinly disguised horror.

'I'll . . . eh . . . just walk up ahead for a while. Look! A rabbit.' And Gordon was off, chasing the startled animal up the lane. With a grunt, his son started after him.

'This is *seriously* wrong!' Mary grabbed Bobby's collar and pulled him back.

'Great.' The boy choked out. 'When *you* start finding things strange I know we're in trouble.'

They caught up with Gordon at Pennywell Cottage. He was hiding behind the garden hedge, just out of sight of the front door.

'C'm'ere. Quick!' He beckoned the children over. 'Stay behind me!'

'Why, what's the matter?' Bobby and Mary crouched beside him, pressed against the thick evergreen foliage. 'There's nobody around.'

'Just wait a minute.' Gordon peered cautiously round the edge of the hedge.

'It's your house, Dad. Nobody's going to bother if we go in the front door. We can climb down the *chimney* if we want.'

'No. Just *wait* a minute.' Gordon held up his hand, like some oddly coiffured commando.

'Hey. I hear a car,' Mary interrupted. It was enough to silence the others. Vehicles weren't a common occurrence on the narrow road that led past Puddledub.

As they watched, a Panda car crested the rise a hundred yards in front of them, coasted down the hill and turned into the driveway of Pennywell Cottage. Bobby's father shrank back, pushing his companions further into the foliage.

'I've got a stick up my nose!' Mary complained.

'Shhhh! Quiet!'

Two police officers got out of the car, went to the front door and knocked. When there was no answer they walked around the house peering in through the windows.

The three onlookers held their breath, pressed as far into the greenery as they could manage. The constables appeared round the other side of the house and headed back to the car.

'C'mon. My wife will have tea on by now.' Constable MacDonald opened the car door. 'Steak pie and chips tonight.'

'Are we coming back tomorrow?' WPC Arnold put her hands on her hips. 'Now *I've* got a feeling about this.'

'Woman's intuition?'

'I believe it's called a hunch when you're in the police force.'

'All right.' MacDonald sighed loudly. 'We'll come back tomorrow. Though I doubt we'll find the whole family murdered inside.'

They got back into the car and drove away.

The hidden figures waited until the sound of the car had faded, then let themselves into the house. Gordon flopped down in his chair, perspiring heavily.

'Oh no! The police aren't looking for you, Dad!' he scoffed, in an uncanny imitation of his son's voice. 'Think *they* came over to borrow a cup of sugar?'

Bobby and Mary took off their coats and stood uncertainly in the middle of the room.

'Hey. You got a message on the answering machine.' There was a flashing red light on the telephone.

'What's an answering machine then?' Gordon lowered his head wearily into his hands. 'All this new technology, you'd think they'd have invented something for zapping someone's head, you know . . . a bringing their memory back kind of thing.'

Bobby pressed a button on the phone.

'Gordon. This is me.' The voice was female and upset and Bobby recognized it immediately. 'Your mobile is switched off so I'm calling to let you know I'm coming round tomorrow night. I've got a late Christmas present for Bobby and I'd like to give it to him in person. And I think we should have a real chat.'

There was a click and the message ended. Bobby's father slowly raised his head.

'Who was that?'

'It's Angelica. Your ex-girlfriend.'

'I have an ex-girlfriend that sounds like *her*?'

'Dad, I don't think we can cover this up much longer.' Bobby sat down next to his father. 'The police will just keep coming back, and Angelica *certainly* won't give up.'

Gordon Berlin rolled his eyes dramatically, but Bobby pressed ahead.

'We haven't got any money left and you can't even remember your PIN number. We just can't go on like this.'

'All right,' his father grumped. 'If my memory isn't back tomorrow we'll go to a doctor. Happy?'

'Thank you.' The boy's relief was obvious. 'Hey. What do you want for tea? I'll make it.'

'Kraft macaroni cheese, please. But don't put any butter or milk in it. I like it all sticky.'

'You want to stay for tea, Mary? It's . . . eh . . . vegetarian.'

'No. I think I'll get home.' The teenager fastened up her coat. 'I hope you feel better tomorrow, Mr Berlin.'

'That's the problem, toots,' Gordon said gaily. 'I feel fine. Just a bit pooped.'

'I'll see you to the door.' Bobby got to his feet.

'No kissing in the hallway!' His father gave a childish snigger.

'Dad!' Bobby blushed bright red and practically pushed Mary out of the living room.

In the hall, the girl quickly shut the door and leaned in close. For a second Bobby thought she really was going to kiss him. He moved his head away, nervously, but Mary's lips stopped next to his ear.

'Why did the dogs at the kennel try to attack your dad? They've never harmed anyone before.'

'*I* don't know.'

'And why did your dad stop at the hedge outside and hide? It's like he *knew* the police were going to turn up.'

'How could he? You're supposed to be the psychic, not him.'

Mary opened the front door. It had grown dark outside and scattered snowflakes danced across the night like frantic stars.

'You know, I quite liked your dad, even if he was a bit miserable.' She stepped into the darkness, pulling her hood over her head.

'But Dodd Pollen is really starting to scare me.'

Chapter 23

Mary walked aimlessly for a long time before finally turning home. A brief flurry of snow had come and gone and now the air was crisp and clear. Stars were strung across the hemisphere like Christmas lights and fire billowed from the chimneys of the ethylene plant, lending the southern sky a bloody tinge.

When she got to her house, the lights were off. In the living room Mary found a note on the coffee table in her grandmother's cramped handwriting.

Gone to bed early, dearie. Had quite a day. Grannie.

'You're not the only one.'

Mary scanned the shelves of Rana's bookcase. There were volumes on gypsy lore, plants and herbs, and dozens of graphic novels and comics. Finally she saw what she was looking for on the top shelf.

The Encyclopaedia of Demonology.

Mary pulled down the volume and sat on her grand-mother's old floral couch. She studied the index for a few moments and then flicked through the pages until she found the chapter she was looking for.

Demonic Possession and Exorcism.

She kicked off her boots, curled her chilly feet underneath her body and began to read.

SIGNS OF DEMONIC POSSESSION

- The victim takes on a different personality.
- The victim often curses a lot, though it is out of character.
- The victim develops an aversion to religious objects, churches, and clergy.
- The victim's personal hygiene changes.
- The victim may become abusive and threatening.
- The victim's diet may change.
- The victim may have a memory blackout.
- The victim's voice may change.
- Animals may be frightened of the victim.

Mary thought of all the things Bobby had told her about his father—and what she had witnessed herself.

She shut the book, chewing her lip.

The passage she had read was a perfect description of Gordon Berlin.

Chapter 24

Bobby scanned the reams he had printed out about amnesia. His father stood in front of the mirror, combing his hair backwards then forwards, trying to hide his receding hairline.

'You think I should put the purple streak back in?'

'Oh, sure. *That* won't attract attention.' Bobby held up the sheet of paper. 'Look. According to this, we need to jog your memory. Find things from your past that you might recognize.'

'All I need is the TV for that.' Gordon tried a side parting. 'They're still showing *Star Trek* and *Dr Who*.'

'I mean personal things.' Bobby glanced up at the ceiling. 'We should try the attic. That's where all the old junk is kept.'

They found the key to the attic, lowered the ladder, and climbed up into the darkness. Bobby switched on the light and his father began opening boxes and trunks like a child at Christmas.

'Hey, there's a kite in this one.' Gordon held up a tatty red rectangle with a paper tail. 'Want to fly a kite sometime?' He tossed the toy aside and delved into another container.

Bobby was staring at a pile of camping equipment in one corner. His father hopped over, a stuffed parrot attached to his shoulder.

'What's up, Bobby me lad?' He squinted at the boy through his half closed fist. 'What do you spy, scurvy knave?'

'My mum and I used to take camping trips around Fife.' Bobby stuck his hands in his pockets. 'We'd eat lunch over that gas stove.'

Gordon dropped the parrot on the floor.

'What was your mother like?' he asked quietly.

'She was wonderful.'

'So . . . why did I leave?'

'I don't know.'

'Neither do I.' Gordon ruffled his son's hair, unsure of how to comfort him. 'Let's keep looking, huh?'

They took opposite sides of the attic and began opening the rest of the boxes. There were more toys, old clothes, and trinkets belonging to Alison Berlin. Gordon's memory might not be getting jogged, but each new find was a fresh jolt for his son.

'You find anything at all?' Bobby suddenly wanted to get out of this dark vault, full of painful reminiscence.

'You better come and look at this, Bobby.'

He hurried over. His father was holding a shoebox full of old photographs.

Bobby took the box and lifted out a handful of yellowing pictures.

'What the . . . ?'

Each photograph was of a boy. In some he was alone. In others he was with a couple who Bobby recognized as Gran and Grandad Berlin.

'Is that me?' Gordon said, shocked.

'I think so.' Bobby felt the hairs rise on the back of his neck. 'It's a bit hard to tell.'

In each photograph the child's face had been obliterated by a thick red pen.

Bobby and his father were both shaken by what they had found. They sat in silence in the living room lost in their own thoughts.

'C'mon. No more sitting round like a couple of bloody pansies,' Gordon said eventually. 'What sort of movies are you into? What's your favourite band? Let's make some toasties and talk about girls.'

Bobby and Gordon spent the rest of the night playing on the X-Box, talking and laughing, eating crisps and drinking Coke. His father had never let him drink Coke before— claiming it was something to do with all big corporations being evil. For a little while, all the unanswered questions were put to the back of their minds and they simply enjoyed each other's company.

By the time they decided to turn in for the night, Bobby had to admit he was starting to have a real affection for Dodd Pollen. More than he liked Gordon Berlin, in fact.

But tomorrow they would go to the nearest hospital and the doctor would cure his father. Bobby hoped that some part of Gordon would remember that he really could have a good time with his son.

As he drifted off, he heard his father call from the next room.

'Goodnight, Bobby boy! Thanks for everything, pal!'

'Goodnight, Dodd!' he called back, then turned over and fell asleep.

Gordon pulled off his T-shirt and went to close the curtains. As he grasped the drapes there was a ping of a small stone hitting the window. He shielded his eyes and squinted through the pane.

There was a shadowy figure in the front garden.

He opened the window and stuck his head out. A man in an overcoat stood on the lawn, smoking a cigarette.

'What you doing out there, mate?' Gordon said in a stage whisper. 'Office party get a little out of hand? You're standing in my garden.'

'You don't know me,' the stranger replied. 'But I know who *you* are.'

'I'm glad somebody does.' Gordon's flippant reply barely masked the unease in his voice.

'I'm here to warn you, Gordon. I think the Lazarus Project has gone wrong.'

'What are you talking about?'

'You don't have to be coy. I'm on my own. I shouldn't even be here.'

'Then get the hell off my lawn.'

'Gordon.' The man looked warily around. 'Tomorrow, I'm going to tell the authorities about you. I can't live with myself unless I do.'

'Oh yeah? Want me to come down and give you a smack in the teeth?' Gordon blustered.

'I know you're bitter, but you have to trust me.' The man nipped the end of his glowing cigarette between two fingers and slid the butt into his pocket. 'I'm serious. You're a danger to too many people and they know exactly where you are.'

He backed down the path, holding up his hands.

'If you want to live through the next few days, you need to either go to the police yourself or get out of here.'

Next morning, Bobby woke refreshed and full of hope. He showered and dressed and took the stairs two at a time.

'Morning, Dad! Want a bagel?'

There was no answer.

In the living room, he found a note under the remote control.

Bobby sat down on the floor, the note dropping from his fingers.

His father was gone.

Had a long think after we went to bed
and I decided that I have to work this
out myself. I know you don't believe it—
but there really are people after me
and I don't want you getting hurt.
You can call the police or tell Angelica,
whoever she is. I don't mind. You need
someone proper to take care of you.

Sorry Bobby.

~~Dodd.~~ Your dad.

[SUNDAY]

Part 3

Helicopters over Fife

Pack up my suitcase, give me my hat
No use to ask me, babe, because I'll never be back
I can't be good no more, once like I did before
I can't be good, baby, honey, because the world gone wrong
– World Gone Wrong, THE MISSISSIPPI SHEIKS

Chapter 25

Mary was having breakfast with her grandmother when she heard hammering on the front door. She opened it to find Bobby Berlin bent over on the step, hands on his knees.

'My dad's missing,' he panted. 'I looked all over and he took my mum's camping equipment from the attic. He's . . . he's run away from home!'

'Camping equipment? Why didn't he just take a bus?'

'He doesn't have any money.' Bobby took a deep breath. 'Anyway, he thinks like a fourteen year old.'

'So do you. You'd take the bus if you were running away.'

'Yeah, but he's totally paranoid. Thinks the authorities are after him, even though they're not.' Bobby shook his head. 'He's trying to walk to Dundee, I just know it.'

'What's all the commotion?'

The children whirled round. Baba Rana was standing in the kitchen doorway wearing a grubby pink robe, her wispy hair up in curlers. She held a mug of coffee in one hand and a lit cigarette in the other.

'It's . . . eh . . . difficult to explain.'

'I got time, dearie.' The old woman patted her white hair daintily. 'I'm not due to meet the queen till my hundredth birthday. Got nothing to do in between.'

'We have to tell someone,' Mary said. 'We can trust my gran.'

'I suppose so,' Bobby replied reluctantly.

Baba Rana smiled pleasantly.

'My dad's had some sort of breakdown, Baba Rana, and he thinks he's my age. He's run away and I have to go after him.'

'Wait. Let me get this straight.' Rana's brow wrinkled even more than usual. 'Your father thinks he's a fourteen-year-old boy?'

'It's worse than that, Gran,' Mary added. 'He thinks he's a completely different person. Somebody called Dodd Pollen.'

'When did this happen?'

'We saw an accident on the railway bridge the other night. Then suddenly he just . . . changed.'

Baba Rana paled.

'Bobby, what did your father look like when he was your age?'

'Eh? I don't know.' Bobby wasn't about to mention that all the photographs of his father as a teenager had been obliterated. 'Point is he's missing.'

'Why don't you call him on his mobile?'

'He left it on the living room table.'

'That was clever.' Mary nodded approvingly. 'The police can track mobile phones. I saw it on some cop show.'

'I bet he's going cross country so he can stay hidden. It wouldn't take more than a couple of days to walk right across Fife.' Bobby shuffled impatiently on the spot. 'But there was a lot of frost during the night, so I can follow his footprints for a few hours at least, till it melts.'

'Since when did you become a big game hunter?' Mary snorted.

'You really need to call the police, sonny.' Baba Rana stubbed out her cigarette in a nearby plant pot. 'This isn't something you can handle on your own.'

'I can persuade him to come back. I know I can.' Bobby backed towards the front door. 'He's just frightened and confused.'

'The police will have a better chance of finding him,' the old woman said sharply.

'I haven't got time to argue. I have to go after him. I'm sorry. I just wanted to let someone know where I'd gone.' Bobby shot Mary an apologetic look, then turned and bolted out of the front door before Rana could talk him into staying longer. Mary ran into the garden and watched him vanish down the lane. Baba Rana followed and put a hand gently on her granddaughter's shoulder.

'Gran?' The girl looked utterly miserable. 'I have to go with him. He's my best friend.'

'Absolutely not, Mary.'

'Bobby needs me. I can . . . I can *feel* it.'

'And I can't let you go chasing some deranged man across Fife. Nor Bobby for that matter. I'm going to call the police.'

'Gran? I think that there's something wrong with Gordon that the police won't understand.'

'What do you mean?' Rana began. But before she could continue she heard an urgent tapping above her head. Looking up, she gave a sharp intake of breath.

There was a figure at her bedroom window. The old woman glanced quickly at her granddaughter, but Mary was still staring down the lane.

'You wait here a minute.' Rana put a finger to her lips and backed into the house. 'I'll be right back.'

When she got upstairs, the boy she had met the day before was sitting on her bed, reading *Chat* magazine. Rana glared at him.

'How exactly did you manage to get up here?'

'I was hiding under the bed.' The boy lowered the magazine and went to the window, peering out from behind the curtain. 'You won't tell, will you?'

Through the window the multiple chimneys of the ethylene plant were visible in the distance. Baba joined the boy in time to see Mary coming back up the path and disappearing indoors.

'But how did you get in?' She lowered her voice so Mary wouldn't hear. 'You might have scared the wits out of my granddaughter.'

'Doesn't sound like it's me Mary has to worry about.'

'I'm a little . . . disturbed by this turn of events.' Rana sat on the bed and patted her bony knees. 'I was walking along and thinking about a headline I'd seen. About the mishap on the bridge. Then suddenly you appeared.' She rubbed her temple. 'Now Bobby says his father changed right after the accident . . . '

She looked sideways at the boy.

'Is it possible?' Rana could hardly believe she was even entertaining the notion. 'Are . . . *you* Gordon Berlin?'

'I don't know,' the boy replied miserably. 'Do I look like him?'

'No. You look like a young boy, not a forty-five-year-old man. Then again Gordon Berlin certainly doesn't look like a fourteen year old called Dodd Pollen.'

'I'm a young boy?'

'Well, of course you are. How could you not know?'

The child nodded towards the mirror.

'I can't see myself.'

Baba Rana followed his eyes and her jaw dropped.

The reflection showed nobody in the room but her.

'I don't feel young.' The boy stood in front of the mirror and stared at the empty image. 'I feel old and lonely.'

'Join the club, dearie.'

The front door slammed. Rana hobbled to the window and looked out. Mary was heading down the lane at a sprint, rucksack over one slim shoulder.

'Stay there,' the old woman cautioned. 'I'm not done with you.'

She descended the stairs as fast as her legs would allow and opened the front door—but Mary was already out of sight.

Baba Rana cursed loudly in Polish. Something she hadn't done in years.

She ran back into the house and dialled 999.

Rana tramped angrily back upstairs but there was no sign of the mysterious boy. Somehow she knew he would be gone. While she waited for the police she put on jeans, a bright purple sweater, and hiking boots. She applied light make-up and lipstick and swept her wispy hair backwards into a ponytail, fastening it with the embroidered red ribbon she had found in her suitcase.

She put on a thick sheepskin jacket and leather gloves, picked up her cigarettes and stuck them in her pocket.

Then the doorbell rang.

Chapter 26

M ary found Bobby at Pennywell Cottage. He was standing in the back garden, hood up, studying the ground.

'Found anything?'

'There are footprints heading in this direction. From the look of them I'd say they belonged to a middle-aged man with a stupid hairstyle, carrying a tent, and wearing engineer boots.'

Mary studied the line of imprints heading away from the house. 'Not bad for an amateur. On the other hand, they're the only set of footprints in the garden.'

'There *is* that.'

'Well then. Let's go after your dad.'

'What do you mean?'

'I'm not letting you do this on your own.' Mary patted her rucksack. 'I've got a sleeping bag, carrots, celery sticks, and two Mars bars.'

'No thanks.' Bobby pulled a face. 'I don't want to get attacked by a herd of rabbits.'

'With your new-found scouting skills you can probably trap one using shoelaces and eat it for lunch.' Mary straddled the garden wall and beckoned to him. 'C'mon. No time to waste.'

'Mary, you can't go with me.' Bobby hung back. 'I really appreciate this and it's great that you want to help, but I have to go alone.'

'I disobeyed my own grandmother to come here. I've never done that in my life.'

'Then go back before you get into even more trouble.'

'Trust me, Bobby. You need me on this trip. And every second you argue your dad is getting further away.' Mary folded her arms, still astride the wall. 'Plus my bum's starting to freeze.'

'You don't understand . . . ' Bobby seemed lost for words. 'I think . . . '

'Come *on*, Bobby.'

'My dad's *changed*.'

'I *had* noticed he's suddenly become a middle-aged punk rocker.'

'That's not what I mean.' Bobby blurted out the words before he had time to change his mind. 'I think he might be *dangerous*.'

'I agree.' Mary slid off the wall. 'For reasons you'd never understand.' She stepped up to her friend and tied the cord of the hood under his chin. 'But for years, all we've really had in this wee place is each other. Whether you like it or not, we're a team and I'm coming with you.'

'You are *so* annoying.' Bobby tugged at the cord of his hood, trying to loosen it before it cut off the blood flow to his head. Then he grinned.

'I bet you put a couple of corned beef sandwiches for me in your bag.'

'Chicken legs actually. I'm your pal, not your personal chef. And I didn't exactly have time to cook a pot roast.' Mary motioned at the footprints. 'We going, or what?'

'All right.' Bobby shouldered his own rucksack. 'Mind you, he's probably stuck in a well or something by now. He's pretty clueless.'

'I wouldn't bet on that,' Mary said ominously. 'We seem to have been doing exactly what he wants the last couple of days. Apart from my gran, nobody else knows about Dodd Pollen.'

They climbed over the garden wall and began walking across the fields.

WPC Arnold and Constable MacDonald sat in Baba Rana's cramped living room with their notebooks out. The air was thick with cigarette smoke. The constables looked at each other.

'Eh . . . this is an interesting story, madam,' WPC Arnold said cautiously.

'Sounds like the ravings of a senile old woman, you mean?' Baba Rana took an aggressive drag on her cigarette and the policewoman cringed. 'But there are two kids out there with a large man who might well be mad as a hatter.

Imagine the trouble you'd be in if you didn't investigate and my story turned out to be true.'

'Remember Berlin's abandoned car?' Constable Mac-Donald nudged his companion. 'I think we should get on this fast. It's not like we have any actual crimes to solve.'

'You any idea where Gordon Berlin might be going?' WPC Arnold asked.

'Dundee. Bobby seemed sure his father was heading for Dundee, but he didn't say why.'

'All right, madam.' The policewoman got to her feet. 'You stay here and we'll contact you as soon as we hear something.'

'Eh? I'd like to come with you and help look.'

'We're professionals, madam. We know what to do.'

'And you've done a fine job keeping down the murder rate in Puddledub. But I know these people and I know the area.'

'I understand your concern.' Constable MacDonald looked suitably embarrassed. 'It's just that we'd be . . . eh . . . a lot faster on our own.'

'We'll find them,' WPC Arnold broke in tactfully. 'Don't worry.'

Baba Rana raised a white eyebrow.

'Finding them might just be the least of your worries,' she muttered.

'You take the car,' WPC Arnold said to her companion once they got outside.

'Where am I going?'

'Doctor Lambert's house. He's the only GP in the area. If Gordon Berlin had any previous mental health problems, Lambert may well know about it. Best if we know exactly what we're dealing with.'

'What are you going to do?'

'I'm going to Pennywell Cottage. See if I can find any clues.'

'What about doctor/patient confidentiality?' Constable MacDonald said archly. 'What about a search warrant?'

'This is Puddledub, not Los Angeles.' WPC Arnold removed her hat and swept a lock of blonde hair off her forehead. 'Let's just use a bit of savvy.'

'You're going to put on a pair of mirrored sunglasses any minute, aren't you?'

'Keep me posted, all right?' WPC Arnold set her cap back on at a jaunty angle and marched off down the road.

'Whoa! Who died and put *you* in charge?' PC MacDonald grunted, getting into the car.

Baba Rana sank into her armchair. The boy's tousled head bobbed up over the back of the couch.

'They gone?'

The woman nearly fell off her seat.

'That is *most* disconcerting. You better not pull that trick when I'm in the bath.'

'They had uniforms,' the boy said. 'They frightened me.'

'That pair?' The woman gave a throaty laugh. 'I doubt

they could find a flag at the top of a pole. They didn't even ask for a description of Gordon Berlin.'

'They live here, Rana. They know what he looks like.'

'All right. But I can't just sit here twiddling my thumbs. And there's only one way to get to Dundee if you're walking.' She stroked her chin thoughtfully. 'You've got to go across the Tay Bridge. If I get a taxi to Inverkeithing, I can catch the train to Dundee and be waiting for them.'

'I'm sure the police will have that covered.'

'I suppose so.' Rana tilted her head back and let out a sigh. Her eyes came to rest on the bookcase.

'What the—?'

She got to her feet, a feeling of dread building in her chest. The books on the top shelf were sticking out slightly.

Rana pulled a chair over and stood on it, with no thought for her own safety this time. She pulled out *The History of Poland* and felt inside the lining.

'Something missing, Rana?'

'A book of Romany spells.' The old woman climbed down, holding her back.

'You don't believe in that stuff, do you?'

'That's a bit rich, coming from an invisible boy.'

She fetched her old rucksack and stomped round the house, throwing in some provisions and a blanket. The boy followed her, chewing on a knuckle.

'You're going to walk?'

'Why not? Gordon and the kids are doing it.' The woman straightened her shoulders. 'I've been tramping these hills for years and I know all the shortcuts. Maybe I can catch up.' She patted the boy on the shoulder. 'You coming, strange little person?'

'I think this is your journey, Rana, not mine.' The boy smiled for the first time since the old woman had met him. 'I hope you find what you're looking for.'

Chapter 27

'Gordon Berlin is a patient of mine, yes.' Doctor Lambert was in his sixties and had a severe stoop. Constable MacDonald wondered if it was a result of a lifetime bending over patients. Short and bald, with a tatty green pullover, Lambert sat behind an enormous oak desk like some shrivelled goblin. 'I can't really give you details of Mr Berlin's medical history, however, as I'm sure you know.'

The constable had been rehearsing his lines on the drive over. He nodded agreeably and took out his notebook.

'I realize that, sir. But I thought, if I gave you a general outline of a hypothetical situation, you would be able to . . . eh . . . comment on what I might be dealing with.' MacDonald coughed politely. 'Hypothetically.'

'Very clever.' Doctor Lambert put on his glasses and went to a large filing cabinet. 'That would be acceptable. Please proceed.'

'We have a situation where a middle-aged man has had some sort of breakdown. We're a bit short on details, but we have the gist of it.'

'Go on.' The doctor knelt beside the cabinet, his knees cracking loudly, and began rummaging through the drawers.

'Well . . . suppose this forty-five-year-old man wakes up and he's convinced he's someone else. What's more, he thinks he's only fourteen. No memory of himself as an adult at all.'

The doctor looked round sharply. 'When did this . . . um . . . theoretical breakdown happen?'

'Couple of days ago.' Constable MacDonald looked at his notebook again, more for show than anything else. After all, he hadn't written any details down.

'Problem is, he's gone missing. And we think his son and a local girl called Mary Mooney might be with him.'

The doctor stood up, holding a large file. He laid it on his desk and pulled out a set of beige folders.

'Gordon Berlin first came to me years ago, at the insistence of his wife. They'd just had a child, Bobby, back then.' The doctor began removing sheets of paper from the folders and spreading them across his desk. Constable MacDonald looked suitably surprised.

'I thought you weren't supposed to divulge medical records.'

'I'm retiring in a year. What are the medical board going to do to me?' Lambert separated files quickly and efficiently, scanning them as he did so.

'Gordon was a likeable man. He was also detached, moody, and a heavy drinker. His wife thought he might be suffering from depression. He didn't want to come to me, but he did it for her.'

'We all get like that sometimes,' the constable said sympathetically. 'Even me. In fact, it's usually the wife's fault.'

'Quite.' The doctor ignored the policeman's attempt at humour. 'But Gordon Berlin seemed different. I couldn't quite put my finger on it.' He held up a sheet of green paper. 'I sent him to Stratheden Hospital for psychological tests. He made a fuss, but he went.'

'What was the result?'

'The hospital psychiatrists weren't sure what to make of him either.' Doctor Lambert sounded uncertain. 'Gordon had a rather . . . eh . . . evasive nature. But these guys don't like to admit to being stumped. In the end they diagnosed him with a condition known as Narcissistic Personality Disorder.'

'And what might that be?' Constable MacDonald was sceptical of personality disorders. He liked good guys to be good and bad guys to be bad. It made arresting them more fun.

'Narcissistic Personality Disorder is a form of sociopathy.'

'You're saying Gordon Berlin is a psychopath?' The constable's eyes widened.

'They're called "People with Antisocial Personality Disorder" these days,' the doctor corrected.

'I don't care if they're called the Nutty Boys, Barmy Army. What are you telling me here?'

'Narcissistic Personality Disorder is often caused by post-traumatic stress—some childhood disaster, for instance. There are several symptoms that only come out later in life.'

'Like eating someone's liver with a nice Chianti?'

'I'd advise you to stop being flippant and start listening.'

'I'm all ears.'

'I can probably write you a prescription for that.' Lambert gave a sharp wheezing laugh. 'Sorry. Couldn't resist it.' He cleared his throat, embarrassed by his burst of uncharacteristic levity, and looked at the notes again.

'The narcissist is arrogant and distant but he often gets away with it because he's also intelligent and charming. But he's not emotionally equipped to deal with other people's needs. He thinks he's special and won't accept other points of view if they don't agree with his. He always has to be right.'

'C'mon, Doc,' Constable MacDonald interrupted. 'I've met lots of people like that. They're called selfish buggers.'

'I'll just finish,' Doctor Lambert said pointedly. 'The narcissist, however, falls apart in times of crisis. He becomes paranoid and may well respond by taking this confusion out on his nearest and dearest.' The doctor looked solemnly over his glasses. 'Let me read you this passage. *The narcissist reserves his most virulent emotions—aggression, hatred, envy—towards those who resemble him the most.*'

The policeman put down his notebook.

'Like his own son?'

'Perhaps.' Doctor Lambert removed the glasses and wiped them on his jacket. 'I'm not an expert in this area. Narcissism wasn't even recognized as a disorder until the nineteen eighties.'

'What *can* you tell me, sir?'

'I think Gordon being diagnosed with such an extreme

condition actually put more of a strain on the Berlin's marriage. He left Fife shortly after that and only came back a year ago, when his wife died.'

'To look after his son?'

'So he said.'

'You didn't believe him?'

'No reason not to. He got a job in the area and the boy looks healthy and well dressed.' The doctor sat back and pressed his fingers together. 'Though I do remember Gordon's exact words, because they were quite unusual.' The man hesitated. 'He didn't exactly say he'd come back to look after his son.'

Constable MacDonald waited.

'He said he'd come back to *save* him.'

'And that didn't sound vaguely . . . creepy to you?'

'I gave the man the benefit of the doubt,' Lambert replied defensively. 'As far as I could see, he'd learned to live with his flaws. He sought me out, of his own accord this time. He seemed determined to do the best he could for his boy.'

'And could you help Mr Berlin?'

'I prescribed Abilify and Risperdal to help him cope. But in the main, it was down to him.'

'So he *was* managing?'

'Absolutely.' A tinge of admiration crept into the doctor's voice. 'He knew there was something wrong with him. He wasn't happy. He was never going to be happy. But he kept a tight rein on his emotions.'

'And now?'

'A sophisticated forty-five year old with a lifetime's experience can handle this disorder. Especially with medication to help him.' The doctor shuffled his notes back into a neat pile. 'A man who believes he is fourteen certainly can't. And if Gordon Berlin has lost his memory, he isn't taking the pills any more. Their effects wear off fast, you know.'

'I don't like the sound of this, Doc.' Constable MacDonald was already on his feet.

'Like I said, I'm no expert,' Doctor Lambert added quickly. 'And the diagnosis the hospital made might even be wrong.'

'And if the diagnosis is right?'

'I doubt he'll be able to keep control of himself for long. He'll quickly develop a sense of mistrust for everyone. Think that people are after him.'

'In that case he'd be right.'

'Then catch him fast. A narcissist with a fourteen-year-old mind and a grown man's strength.' The doctor took a long, deep breath. 'That would make Gordon Berlin very dangerous indeed.'

Chapter 28

WPC Arnold walked round Pennywell Cottage twice. The lights were off and there was no sign of life. She stood on the front step ringing the bell yet again. There was no response.

'I don't suppose . . . ' She turned the handle and the door swung open.

This was a bit of a dilemma for she knew she wasn't supposed to enter without a warrant. WPC Arnold smoothed down her uniform and thought hard.

'Last time we met in the pub, Gordon, we got a little tipsy,' she said to herself. Actually they had both got raving drunk. 'And you told me I could come round and have a bottle of wine any time I liked. Well. Here I am.'

She stepped into the hall.

First she checked for signs that Baba Rana's story was true. There was no food in the fridge, only several bottles of wine, but that didn't prove anything. There was no sign of a note from Gordon Berlin, but Bobby might have kept that. There were two mobile phones on the living room table, father's and son's she supposed, but she couldn't understand why they had left them in the house. WPC Arnold went upstairs and checked the bedrooms, but found nothing unusual there either.

That left the attic.

The dusty top room was filled with dark angular shapes. There was an overhead bulb without a shade and, when the policewoman switched it on, the light revealed a treasure trove of useless objects. Teddy bears, a rocking horse, boxes and crates, a cricket bat—all the paraphernalia that accumulated when lives moved on but couldn't let go. Most of this was thickly overlaid with dust, but criss-crossing footprints and open boxes showed that somebody had been up here very recently.

In one corner was a pile of camping equipment and, here, there was evidence that some of the items had been dragged across the floor and through the attic doorway.

'So you *are* going cross country.'

Now she had something to fasten on to. Wherever the dust was disturbed, these objects had been newly touched—including a stuffed parrot lying in the middle of the floor.

WPC Arnold went to the nearest crate and shone her torch inside. On top of a pile of clothes was an old shoebox containing dozens of faded photographs of a young boy. Judging by the square shape of the snapshots and the thickness of the paper, they had been taken many years ago. The policewoman flipped through them, a frown on her face. Each photograph was mutilated and bent, scribbled over with a bright red crayon until the face was totally obscured. The policewoman sat back.

'I don't know what I'm looking at, but I'm not liking it at all.'

She got up and glanced around. There was an antique desk shoved under one of the eaves with a drawer pulled open. The lock looked as if it had been forced.

WPC Arnold strode over and crouched beside the desk.

The lock *was* broken and the drawer was empty. Almost.

At the back were three shell casings. And there was a bald patch on the bottom of the drawer—the outline clearly showing what had been there.

'Oh my God.' WPC Arnold stared at the imprint. 'Gordon Berlin's got a gun.'

Chapter 29

WPC Arnold ran down the stairs and round to the back garden. The frost-bitten grass was mashed down by footprints but she soon found what she was searching for. On the other side of the garden wall three sets of tracks led across the fields.

She pulled out her walkie-talkie. It didn't have a huge range but Doctor Lambert's house was only a few miles away. She should be able to reach Constable MacDonald.

'MacDonald, this is WPC Arnold. I'm at Pennywell Cottage. Where are you? Over.'

'In the car, heading in your direction.' The familiar voice sounded strained. 'I'm only a couple of minutes away. Over.'

'We're going to need back-up. The two children have gone in the same direction as Gordon Berlin and he may be armed and possibly dangerous.'

'Oh, he's dangerous all right. I'll be there soon.'

WPC Arnold had worked with Constable MacDonald on and off for years. She could tell from the policeman's clipped delivery that something was very wrong.

'I think you should radio for assistance right now. I'm going to follow the tracks and see if they intersect a road where you can pick me up. Over.'

'That's a negative, Constable,' MacDonald retorted. 'You're to stay there until I arrive. Over.'

'Who says?' WPC Arnold bristled, forgetting radio protocol.

'The Chief Inspector of Fife Constabulary, that's who. I'm to pick you up and we're to head for police headquarters at Methil.' Before WPC Arnold could protest, the radio went dead.

The policewoman strode up and down the garden, fuming. She kicked at frosted blades of grass, checked her handcuffs and glared indignantly up the lane until the Panda car appeared over the crest of the hill. It drew to a halt in Pennywell's drive.

Constable MacDonald didn't get out. He stayed in the driver's seat, staring stolidly through the windscreen, his hands gripping the steering wheel.

'Are you crazy?' WPC Arnold pulled open the door and leaned inside, her face red. 'Gordon Berlin has a gun! We need to go after them.'

'Yes. I radioed that information in a minute ago.' Without looking round, Constable MacDonald held out the handset of the police radio. 'The Chief Inspector wants a word.'

His companion snatched the receiver and held it to her ear.

'WPC Arnold here. Sir, we have a potentially critical situation developing. Over.' She wasn't sure of the correct terminology for a state of affairs like this, but felt she sounded suitably urgent.

'This is Chief Inspector Montgomery,' the radio crackled. 'You are to proceed to Methil police station immediately.'

WPC Arnold couldn't believe what she was hearing.

'Sir!' she objected. 'We are following a white male, Gordon Berlin, who is probably mentally ill and who may well be armed!'

'I realize the seriousness of the situation, Constable.' The Chief Inspector's voice also had a tense quality to it. 'But this is *not* something we can discuss over the radio.'

'With all due respect, sir, this man may have two children with him!'

'You listen to me.' Her superior's tone turned glacial. 'You and Constable MacDonald are to make no attempt to pursue Gordon Berlin. You hear me? You are to return immediately to headquarters and await further orders. Do you understand?'

'No, sir. I *don't* understand.'

'And I don't care,' the Chief Inspector replied menacingly. 'You get back here *now*!'

WPC Arnold climbed into the car and replaced the headset, shaking with fury. Constable MacDonald was still staring ahead, gripping the steering wheel as if it were about to be wrenched from his grasp.

'Before you ask, no, I've no idea what just happened.' He slammed the car into reverse. 'Put your seat belt on.'

He whirled the Panda round and headed back the way he had come.

Chapter 30

Bobby and Mary had been following Gordon's foot-prints for almost two hours. Bobby's father had crossed over a couple of minor roads and, each time, the pair had managed to find his trail on the other side. But the frost was dissipating fast.

'This is hopeless,' Bobby moaned. 'We've almost reached Cowdenbeath. 'There's no way we can follow him once he gets there.'

'If he's paranoid, then he's hiding from everyone, and he doesn't know the way,' Mary replied confidently. 'We must be moving faster than him. He could be just over the next hill.'

'How does he even know where Dundee is? Signposts won't be any help, because he's not following any roads.'

'Maybe there was a map in your mum's camping stuff.'

'Nah. My mum knew every inch of Fife. Mind you, she had a compass.'

'That might be what he's using.' Mary looked up at the pale sun. 'He's been heading directly north the whole time.'

She punched her companion in the arm. 'C'mon. When we lose his trail, then we can give up. But we haven't yet, have we?'

'Oh, you're so damned chirpy about everything. We've as much chance of finding my dad as I have of winning the lottery.'

'That's because you don't play the lottery,' Mary said with infuriating good humour. 'My gran buys me a ticket every week.'

And, sure enough, they found Bobby's father ten minutes later.

Gordon was sitting at the edge of a small wood, looking across at the town of Cowdenbeath, a large rucksack by his feet and a book open over his crossed knees. He threw his hands in the air when he spotted the children.

'What the hell are you two doing here?' he said belligerently. 'How did you find me?'

Bobby was tired and cold and in no mood for such an inhospitable reaction.

'See this stuff all over the ground?' He swept his hand round in an arc. 'It's frost. You leave footprints in it, no matter how sneakily you bugger off from home.'

'I never thought of that.' His father looked down at his feet. 'I suppose I'm a real city boy.' His head shot up and he checked the area behind the teenagers. 'What if you're being followed?'

Mary nodded towards Cowdenbeath—grey, smoky, and

spread across their path. 'As soon as we cross that, there won't be any footprints to follow.'

'Mary!' Bobby swiped at the girl. 'We're not carrying on. We're all going home. Together!'

'You two *should* go back.' Gordon agreed. 'But I just can't.'

'Listen, Dad.' Bobby sat down beside his father. 'If you're worried about the police, I *know* they're not interested in you.'

'Yeah? How do you figure that?'

'Because you go drinking with the local policewoman. It was her we saw earlier at the cottage.'

'Really? You think she's been spying on me?'

'What? By sitting with you in a bar! The police just want to know why you left your car at Aberdour station. All they'll do is insist you see a doctor.'

'Which isn't bad advice, really,' Mary added tentatively.

'Then what? They'll lock me up in a looney bin! And they'll make *you* go and stay in a home or something, because I can't look after you!' Gordon picked up the book he had been reading and thrust it at his son. 'The place I need to go is here!'

Bobby looked at the picture his father was holding out. It was an old black and white photograph of Dundee, taken from the Fife side of the Tay, with the railway bridge in the foreground.

'I *recognize* this place, Bobby,' his father urged. 'I *remember* it. I can't stop looking at the picture.' He shut the book with a snap. 'I have to keep going. The answer to what happened to me is there, I just know it.'

'We *could* get to Dundee, you know.' Mary sat down too. 'It's only a day and a half to the River Tay. And if Mr Berlin's memory doesn't come back . . . '

'Then I really *will* see a doctor,' Gordon finished. 'And don't call me Mr Berlin, eh? It creeps me out.'

'You guys are insane.' Bobby looked from one to the other in frustration.

Mary rubbed at her nose. 'I just got a fee—'

'And don't tell me you've got a feeling about it!'

'Well, I have.'

'A day and a half, eh?' Gordon gave his most disarming smile. 'It's not long. Anyway, I can't get into worse trouble than I am now.'

'All right. All right! But we're coming with you.'

'I don't mind.' His father grinned. 'The countryside is a scary place when you're on your own.'

'Eh, Mr Berlin . . . Dodd . . . ' Mary began.

'Call me Gordon.' Bobby's father patted his son on the shoulder. 'The name Dodd upsets old sourpuss here.'

'Why have you stopped?' Mary ignored Bobby's scowl.

'Someone put a town in the way.' Gordon pointed to Cowdenbeath. '*That's* not in my book.'

'What is this anyway?' Bobby picked up the slim volume and read the front cover.

The Lost Railways of Fife.

'I found it in the house. It's got maps and everything.' Gordon looked puzzled. 'Didn't say anything about a bloody great town. I don't want to go into a town.'

'This book is about railway lines that existed over a

hundred years ago.' Bobby slammed the book shut. 'That's why it's called *lost* railways. There's thousands of people living in these parts now—we're not in the Sahara Desert.'

'It's the only map I could find.' Gordon nudged Mary conspiratorially. 'Was he this cheeky to me when I was a proper dad?'

Bobby sniffed disdainfully and Mary knew what he was thinking. As far as she could tell, Gordon Berlin had *never* been a proper dad. She thought it best to change the subject.

'Actually, once we get past Cowdenbeath, we *can* avoid towns and villages all the way to Dundee. We can cut round Loch Leven, and head through the Lomond Hills into Eden forest. If we camp there for the night, we can travel up to Newburgh on the banks of the Tay the next day. Then we follow the river to the bridge. Dundee is on the other side but the Fife bank is virtually uninhabited. If we're careful, I bet we can reach the city without seeing anyone.'

'Sounds like a plan to me.' Bobby's father got to his feet. 'Let's get through this horrible town as quick as possible and back into the countryside.' He winked at Bobby. 'You up for an adventure, pal?'

'Whatever.' His son gave a heartfelt sigh. 'But I don't get the cloak and dagger stuff. I really don't. There's nobody after us.'

'Hey, what's that noise?' Mary held up her hand. 'Sounds like . . . '

'I hear it.' Bobby looked up. 'It's coming from above.'

'Into the trees. Quick!' Gordon grabbed the children by the hoods of their coats and hauled them effortlessly to their feet. He spread both burly arms wide and herded them into the woods. They collapsed on the grass as the noise reached deafening proportions.

'Up there!'

Through the branches they could see dozens of fat shapes drifting through the air. Then dozens more.

'Helicopters.' Bobby shouted over the ululating rotors. 'I've never *seen* so many helicopters. And they're *huge*.'

The fleet of flying giants cleared the edge of the woods and floated north over Cowdenbeath, growing smaller until they sank below the horizon.

Bobby's father turned to his son, a fierce look in his eyes.

'Still think nobody's looking for me, smart guy?'

Bobby and Mary were too stunned to reply.

Chapter 31

The North Sea
30 miles off the coast of the Shetland Islands

Eddie Hall was dozing on his bunk when he heard shouting from the captain's cabin next door. The skipper and the first mate, it seemed, were having a fine old barney.

Eddie groaned and put the pillow over his head. He had been given the dawn watch and now he was exhausted—but the argument was too loud and too close for him to ignore. Giving up, he lay on his back and tried to make out what was being said.

'I already told you, I've been contacted by our buyer,' Captain Morrison said loudly. 'Instead of mooring off the north of Scotland, we're going to keep going right down the coast, into the River Tay almost up to Newburgh. The pick-up point will be there.'

'Are you insane?' Salvesson shouted back. 'You'll kill us all!'

Eddie's eyes opened wide at that. The first mate was a gloomy man and prone to exaggeration, but he sounded more agitated than the crewman had ever heard him.

'Do you have any idea what this consignment is worth?' the captain roared. 'Salvesson, we're fishermen—we take risks every day!'

'We're not fishermen any more,' the first mate replied scathingly. 'Skipper, we can't land *anywhere* with this cargo! We have to stay at sea!'

'We are heading for the River Tay and that is a direct order from your captain.'

Salvesson uttered something in Norwegian and Eddie didn't need a translator to tell that it was highly uncomplimentary. He heard the cabin door slam against the wall and footsteps thumping along the passage, up the ladder, and onto the deck. A few seconds later a second set marched past. With a fatigued moan, he turned over on his side, hand brushing against the tin flute by his head. Eddie drifted back into an uneasy sleep, Salvesson's last words to him still echoing round the young sailor's head.

The Lillian Gish *is doomed.*

He woke again two hours later, hauled himself from the bunk and went up on deck. It was mid afternoon and, despite the fact that it was December, there wasn't a cloud in the sky. Captain Morrison was in the wheelhouse, steering a southerly course.

'Everything OK, Skipper?'

'What makes you ask?' The captain didn't turn round.

'I . . . eh . . . heard you and the first mate arguing. You said you were heading for the River Tay and he didn't like it.'

'You heard right. We're heading for the Tay.'

'But trawlers don't operate from that area. Won't the coastguard be suspicious if they see us?' Eddie didn't like questioning his superior, but this didn't make sense. 'The first mate didn't seem to think it was a good idea.'

'Salvesson is gone,' Captain Morrison said. 'I set him ashore at the Shetland Islands while you were asleep.' His steely gaze fastened on Eddie. 'I won't take insubordination aboard my ship. Understand, Mr Hall?'

Eddie was stunned.

'Can two people operate this ship?'

'It'll be difficult, but we'll manage.' Captain Morrison checked his compass, his hands now steady as a rock. 'As long as you do exactly what I say.'

Eddie noticed something out of the corner of his eye.

'What happened to the radio?'

The black box lay on its side on the wheelhouse floor, a huge dent in its side.

'The first mate and I got into a little scuffle. The radio got broken.' Morrison stood toe to toe with the crewman and stared down, unblinking, into his eyes. 'Another reason I put him ashore. You got a problem with that?'

The captain was a large, solid man and Eddie's head only came level with his chest. With his bushy black beard and fiery red eyes, the irate skipper looked like some old-time pirate. Eddie hoped there wasn't a plank hidden some-where on the *Lillian Gish*.

'No problem, sir.'

'Good.' Captain Morrison gave his companion a hefty

slap on the arm. 'And now we share the money fifty-fifty, eh? Greater risk but a *huge* reward. You could cruise round the world instead of working on a tub like this. You could really live, son.'

'Aye aye, Skipper.' Eddie glanced at the broken radio again.

'Then get below and check the engines.' Captain Morrison tapped the compass. 'I want this ship moving at full speed until we reach our destination.'

Eddie left the wheelhouse and went below deck, his stomach churning. He didn't understand why the first mate had been so desperate to keep the ship at sea—but there was no doubt that he *had*. So why would he agree to get off at the Shetland Islands? And how come the engines stopping hadn't wakened Eddie? He'd been on the *Lillian Gish* long enough to be disturbed by any change in the rhythm of its turbines.

Eddie Hall had the horrible suspicion that Lasse Salvesson hadn't been put ashore at all. That, instead, Captain Morrison had granted the first mate's wish in the most horrific way.

Lasse Salvesson, Eddie feared, would be staying at sea permanently.

Chapter 32

Despite Gordon's misgivings, the trio breezed through Cowdenbeath without incident. Bobby even stopped at a shop and got bottles of water and some sandwiches with the little money they managed to pool together. Nobody looked at them. Nobody talked to them. And before they knew it they were out the other side of the town and heading across the fields.

This put Bobby's father in fine spirits and he treated his companions to a loud rendition of 'Anarchy in the UK' as he walked. It was kind of embarrassing to listen to a grown man warbling a punk rock anthem at the top of his voice, so Bobby marched on ahead, leaving his father and Mary behind.

After a while, Gordon stopped singing.

'So, what's the twenty-first century really like? I asked Bobby but he just said "hellish".'

'He can be a bit negative,' Mary conceded. 'But you must have some idea of what's going on in the world. You've had nothing to do except surf the net and watch TV.'

'Yeah, but I mostly watched *Sponge Bob Squarepants*. I always found the news boring.'

The girl thought for a while. 'Well . . . There's been all sorts of new inventions, like cloning and . . . eh . . . plastic surgery.'

'I like the internet,' Gordon said enthusiastically. 'Have you got a computer? I could email you when this is over.'

'We can't afford one,' the girl replied regretfully.

'Bobby says that everyone in the Middle East hates us and there's going to be a religious war.'

'Yes, he would say something like that.'

'He thinks that overcrowding and pollution is destroying the world and that big oil companies are to blame. He says something called global warming is going to wipe out the earth. It isn't true is it?'

'Bobby always expects the worst about everything.' Mary scratched her ear uncomfortably. 'It's just the way he is.'

'That's a stupid way to be.' Gordon let the cold air fill his lungs. Then he let out a shuddering breath.

'He got that attitude from me. Didn't he?'

'I don't know.' Mary glanced guiltily at the man walking beside her. 'But I think so.'

Gordon nodded to himself; his mouth turned down so firmly that deep lines dissected either side of his bristled chin. He stuck his hands in his pockets and trudged ahead of his companion, gathering speed as he walked.

He spotted his son cresting the rise of the next hill, looking small and alone. By this time Gordon was perspiring heavily and his gelled-up hair was flattened to his forehead.

'Hold on there, Bobby boy!' he shouted, breaking into a sprint. But the camber was steep and the ground uneven. By the time he reached his son, he was gasping for air. His chest felt as if it was encased in iron bands.

Bobby was sitting on the crest of the hill, his back to a rock, eating an apple. Reaching him, Gordon sank to his knees, puffing like a pair of bellows. His son knelt beside him, concern etched across his face.

'You OK, Dad?'

'My . . . lungs are on fire and . . . my legs feel like they're being boiled in oil.' His father rolled onto his back, eyes closed and chest heaving. 'Didn't I ever do any bloody exercise?'

'Well, you walked to the pub three times a week.' Bobby picked up a blade of grass and rolled it between his fingers. 'With the amount of staggering you did coming back, you must have covered a fair few miles.'

His father opened one eye and propped himself up on his elbow.

'You believe in second chances, Bobby?'

'What do you mean?'

'I mean, when I get my memory back I'm going to treat you proper,' Gordon announced solemnly. 'I'm going to be a better dad. I promise.'

'What makes you think you were a bad dad?' Bobby glanced accusingly at the far off figure of Mary, labouring up the slope towards them.

'You do.' His father pulled off his rucksack and sat up, still struggling for breath. 'You're lonely and angry . . . and you hate the world and that didn't happen overnight.' He furrowed his brow, desperately trying to remember. 'I was like that too, Bobby. At least, I *think* so.'

His son bit furiously into the apple, looking the other way.

'The funny thing is, I don't feel alone now.' Gordon patted his chest. 'I just feel like I'm going to have a heart attack.' He chuckled to himself. 'But I'm happy because of *you*.'

He gave a beaming smile.

'I just feel that, for the first time, I've got a family that I care about and who cares about me.'

Bobby sniffed loudly. The sudden lump in his throat wasn't caused by the apple.

'When you get your memory back you should give up smoking,' he said gruffly.

Gordon lay back and stared up at the sky.

'Right now, I'd happily give up breathing altogether.'

Mary crested the hill to find Bobby lying beside his father, laughing uncontrollably. Gordon was giggling and coughing, his sweaty face bright red.

'Bobby was wondering how we're going to find a school uniform to fit me,' he sniggered. 'You know? If my memory doesn't come back?'

'What? Is the air really thin up here or something?' Mary shook her head in bemusement. 'Lack of oxygen must have gone to your brains.'

'He'll make a great playground bully though, won't he?' Bobby guffawed.

'We'd better get moving. And we should do it now.'

'Don't tell me . . . ' Bobby wagged a finger at her. 'You've got a feeling.'

'Very amusing.' Mary gave her friend a swift kick in the leg. 'No. It's because you and the world's biggest schoolboy here can be spotted ten miles away if you stay on top of this hill.'

'Yeah, you idiot.' Gordon gave his son a friendly punch in the arm. The impact almost knocked the boy over. 'We're coming, Mary. It's all Bobby's fault.'

'Aye, right.' The girl pointed to the rolling green farmland sloping away in front of them. 'Come on. It's all downhill from here.'

'There's no need to be so pessimistic.' Still laughing, Bobby threw his apple core at Gordon who caught it and pitched it back. It bounced off his son's shoulder and hit Mary on the back of the head, prompting another round of hysteria.

'Boys,' she muttered, heading into the valley. 'They never grow up.'

Chapter 33

The northern half of Fife was sparsely populated compared to the south and the trio were able to cross open country without fear of encountering a soul. Even so, Gordon Berlin's actions were becoming worryingly erratic. He approached the top of every hill at a crouch and frequently scanned the dusky sky for signs of aerial surveillance.

'I don't think those helicopters were looking for you,' Bobby tried to reassure him. 'There's an airbase at Leuchars and that's only about thirty miles from here. They were probably on a training exercise.'

'Dozens of them? Is that common round these parts?'

'To be honest, I've never seen so many helicopters,' his son admitted. 'In fact I've never seen more than one in the air at a time.'

'I've never seen that many *birds* in the air,' Mary added unhelpfully.

'Then we'll stick as close to cover as we can.' Gordon glanced upwards again. 'Just in case.'

'We'll have to think about stopping for the night.' Mary looked at her watch. 'The sun will be setting soon and we can't go anywhere after that.'

'I've got a torch.' Bobby's father pulled a MagLite the size of his little finger from his rucksack.

'So have I, but it's going to get really dark and our torches won't light up more than a couple of metres. I don't fancy falling into a quarry or breaking my leg in some rabbit hole.'

The others could see her point. The sky was already a deep purple and the fields stretching in front of them were taking on an inky hue.

'Where do you think we should camp?' Gordon bowed to Mary's superior knowledge of the area. She took a folded map from one pocket and her own torch from another.

'The A91 is a couple of miles up ahead. It's the last big road between us and the river Tay.' She turned on the torch and shone it over the map so the others could see properly. 'It'll be dark when we get there—the best time to cross it without being noticed. Just beyond that is an abandoned railway line. We should be able to follow it, even in the dark, until we come to the old Pitlour station.'

'That's in my book!' Bobby's father flicked through the pages. 'It's used to load ore from the local mine.'

'Maybe a century ago. But now the mine is gone and the station is derelict. It's miles from the nearest village, so it's the perfect place to camp.'

'Sounds like a plan.' Gordon raised his hand. 'All those for Mary's idea, say "aye". Those against say "I'm a big fat pansy".'

'You're obviously a natural born leader,' Bobby grunted.

'Have you noticed something odd about the skyline?' Mary was staring at the horizon. 'Doesn't it seem a strange colour?'

'That's the sun setting, isn't it?'

'The sun sets in the west, Mr Berlin.' Mary switched off her torch and they could all see an orange tinge shimmering in the sky.

'The light's coming from the north.'

She was right. An hour later it was pitch black, apart from the weird glow over the hills, and the trio found themselves stumbling every few feet.

'The A91 must be on the other side of this rise,' Mary said confidently. 'I can hear cars.'

'Me too.' Bobby stopped and listened. 'But they sound funny. Like they're just revving their engines. Like they're not moving.'

'I can hear voices.' Bobby's father stopped walking as well.

'Are they in your head?'

'Very funny. You sure there isn't another town up ahead?'

'Not according to the map. Anyway, we'd see street lamps and windows.'

'Put your torches off and stay behind me.' Gordon waved the children back. 'Something's not right.'

The party struggled up the last hundred yards of the rise. Now they could clearly make out the sound of engines and

179

shouting too, though they couldn't hear what was being said.

'Stay low.' Bobby's father crouched down. 'Let's see what the hell's going on.'

They crawled over the crest of the rise. Gordon gave a horrified whimper.

Below them the A91 was strung end to end with cars, bright headlights and red tail-lights stretching as far as they could see. The vehicles were inching along at little more than walking pace.

But that wasn't the worst part. Threading their way through the slow moving column were groups of soldiers. As they drifted in and out of the headlights Bobby could see they were armed. Behind the nightmare scene, the northern sky still glowed a faint orange.

'What in the name of holy hell is this?' Bobby's father held back the teenagers. 'Is everyone in the bloody world looking for me?'

Mary and Bobby shook their heads uncomprehendingly.

'We can't get past that,' Gordon said despairingly. 'It's chock-a-block. Should we wait until morning?'

'If it's still like this at daybreak we'll never get by without being seen. Our best chance is to cross now.'

'Excuse me!' Bobby piped up. 'Isn't anybody wondering what's actually going *on* down there? Where did all these cars come from?'

'We won't find that out sitting in the dark.' Mary stood up. 'We need to ask the people on the road.'

'Are you nuts?'

'Look. The cars are moving so slowly that half the folk have got out. Nobody is going to notice another three people in the dark.' She shouldered her rucksack and moved forward. 'We'll mingle with them, find out what's happening, then take off.'

'This is something to do with me,' Gordon whispered.

'Not this time, Dad. This is a much bigger deal than hunting for one guy on the run. I hate to say it, but Mary's right. We need to find out what's going on.'

Gordon's eyes darted right and left. Then he nodded a reluctant agreement.

The trio made their way unsteadily downhill towards the road, taking small careful footsteps and clutching each other for support.

They stopped a few yards from the road, still invisible against the black background of the hill. Now they could see the soldiers were British troops. They seemed to be trying to keep the passengers inside their vehicles and the column moving. Some cars had the windows rolled down and they could hear people crying inside. To their left several drivers and passengers had got out and were arguing with the soldiers, but the details of their angry conversations were lost in the thrum of a hundred idling engines. The air was thick with exhaust fumes.

'Take our hands.' Bobby reached out to his father. 'And remember that *one* of us is supposed to be an adult.'

By now Gordon was almost rigid with fear. He clasped both children's hands and squeezed tightly. They moved onto the road.

An officer turned from the argument as they stepped onto the tarmac.

'You three! Where did *you* just appear from?'

'We needed to go to the toilet, sir,' Bobby shouted back. 'We were desperate, so my dad took us off the road for a minute.'

'I understand, but please return to your vehicle. We have to keep this column moving.' The officer rubbed his temple, fatigue etched across his face. 'If your car holds the line up you *will* be towed off the road.'

'Sorry!' Gordon shook himself out of his terrified torpor. 'Our BMW is just back there . . . eh . . . somewhere.'

'Then get going. And stay inside it from now on.' The officer turned back to his men and Gordon heaved a sigh of relief.

'Let's get right across and out the other side,' he hissed.

'But we still don't know what's happening.' Bobby let go of his hand. 'You two head back down the line a bit and cross the road. I'm going to talk to the driver of one of the cars and then catch you up.'

'Then hurry, for God's sake.'

'Bobby.' Mary nodded her head in the direction of the soldiers. 'Look out.'

The officer had stopped talking to his men, and was staring at them. He pulled a crumpled sheet of paper from his pocket, unfolded it and held it up. His expression changed.

'Excuse me, sir!' he barked at Bobby's father. 'Are you Gordon Berlin?'

'Dammit!' Gordon almost jerked Mary off her feet. 'Run!'

'Mr Berlin!' The officer moved towards him, waving for his men to follow. 'Please. Stop now!'

Gordon ignored him, dodging round cars, still holding Mary's hand. Bobby cursed silently to himself and scuttled after them.

As Gordon and Mary reached the edge of the road, a soldier rose up from one of the vehicles where he had been talking to the occupants. Leaping forward, he spread his arms wide to block their path.

'I've got him, sir!'

Bobby's father swung Mary away. The girl sprawled across the asphalt, skinning her hands and knees. Gordon deftly sidestepped the oncoming soldier, grabbed the man's wrist, and jerked hard, slamming the surprised assailant into the side of the nearest vehicle. The soldier reached for the gun slung over his shoulder but Gordon elbowed him viciously in the face. The man fell back against the car again and slid to the ground, blood spurting from his broken nose.

Bobby ducked behind a black Nissan and fumbled in his rucksack. The officer and his men were only a few feet away now, one or two sliding across the bonnets of cars in their attempt to get to their quarry.

His father's face had contorted into a mask of rage. Raising his boot, he brought it down on the soldier's chest with all his strength. Still running, the officer fumbled for the revolver holstered at his waist. Gordon lashed out with his foot again, his eyes filled with a terrible fury.

There was a deafening report from behind the Nissan and the soldiers skidded to a halt. Gordon's head jerked up, teeth bared, like a cornered animal.

Bobby was holding a pistol, the smoking barrel pointed into the air. Before the soldiers could react he levelled the gun at the officer.

'Let my dad go, or I'll shoot.'

'Don't be stupid, son.' The officer held up his hands. 'We just need to talk to your father.'

'No. He *said* the authorities were looking for him!' Bobby backed towards the side of the road. 'And I didn't believe him!'

Gordon staggered towards Mary, his eyes still wild. He reached down and pulled the girl to her feet.

'We just want a word with your dad,' the officer said gently. 'There's no need for this.'

'Don't trust him, Bobby!' Gordon snarled maniacally. 'Make them let me go!'

'Then get moving!' The boy's voice was ragged. 'Run!'

His father turned and dragged Mary forcibly off the road and into the darkness. Bobby backed after them, still pointing the pistol at the officer. When he reached the edge of the road he turned and bolted down the incline. One soldier yanked a rifle from his shoulder and took aim.

'Don't be stupid, man.' The officer slapped the weapon up. 'He's hardly more than a child. Send a group of squaddies after them and get me a radio. Use extreme caution and I don't want to hear any shooting.'

'I don't think we'll find them, sir. We were rushed out

here so fast, we weren't issued with night vision equipment. We've only got three torches between the whole squad.'

'Dammit!' The officer slammed his hand on the bonnet of the nearest car and the frightened occupants recoiled in terror. 'Let them go then.'

'Sir?'

'I doubt Gordon Berlin would be useful to us anyway. I got a call from top brass a short while ago and, according to the local police force, he's lost his memory.'

'Talk about bad luck, eh, sir?'

'Bad luck is breaking a mirror.' His superior stuffed the paper back into his pocket. 'This is a damned catastrophe.'

'It is for *him*.' The soldier shouldered his rifle. 'He and those kids are heading right towards the danger zone.'

'I know,' the officer replied resignedly. 'But there are only three of them. We've got hundreds of people to save right here.'

'Yes, sir.' The soldier beckoned to two of his companions. 'Gutsy kid though.'

'Aye. He is.' The officer looked at the orange tinge over the northern hills. 'But that won't help where *he's* going.'

Chapter 34

Gordon and Mary raced through the night, hand in hand, stumbling and falling every few feet.

'Stop, will you?' the girl pleaded. 'Stop before we break our necks!'

'They're not going to catch me!' Gordon tugged the girl forward again.

'Mr Berlin, you're hurting me!' Mary dug her feet into the soft ground. 'Please! Please! Look behind you. There are no torches anywhere! Nobody's coming after us!'

With an effort she shook loose the man's grip and Gordon sank to his knees.

'Why not?' he gasped, trying to quieten his staccato breathing. 'You saw what happened! They almost had me!'

'Calm down!' Mary grabbed the man by the arms. 'Try and think logically!'

'I'm too scared!'

'The soldiers were there to keep that line of cars moving, that's all. They haven't come after us!'

'You heard the officer. He knew who I was!'

'Yes he did. But he seemed to be the only one.' She gripped Gordon's arms tighter, trying to stop him rising to his feet. 'I don't understand what's going on, but it's obvious that the army's priority is that traffic jam. It looked like some sort of evacuation.'

'Can we crawl for a while? Just a few hundred yards.'

'We can't see our hands in front of our faces! If we *are* being chased, the soldiers will have less chance of finding us if we stay absolutely still.'

'You're right. Sorry. Sorry for knocking you over too.' The man began to cough, hand clutching his chest. 'I kind of lost it back there.'

'I'm all right. My knees sting a bit, but that's all.'

'What about Bobby? Where *is* he?'

'I don't know.' Mary sounded less confident now. 'He'd probably spot us if we turned on our torches, but so would the soldiers.'

'That was *so* cool the way he saved us.' Gordon's voice was filled with admiration. 'Where did he get a *gun*?'

'Yes.' Mary's tone was altogether less complimentary. 'I'd like to ask him that too.'

They sat in silence for a few minutes, surrounded by blackness, listening. They could still hear engines idling in the distance but nothing closer disturbed the stillness. No troops. No Bobby.

'I'm getting cold.'

'Me too.'

'What are we going to do?'

'Well, we can't go back, not now your son's declared war

182

on the whole British army.' Mary reached out and took Gordon's hand. 'But Bobby knows where we were going to camp. Let's find that railway line and follow it to the station.'

'Will he think of that too?' Gordon sounded doubtful.

'He hasn't done anything right so far,' Mary replied contemptuously. 'But we can live in hope.'

Like so many of the choices she'd made in her long life, Baba Rana had no clear idea why she opted to walk to Dundee, rather than take a bus or train. Perhaps it was because Mary was going cross country and she wanted to stay as close to her granddaughter as possible. How she could help, if the girl got into difficulties, was beyond her. Nor was she particularly confident of being able to catch up with two healthy teenagers. Even if Gordon Berlin was with the children, slowing them down, he was still thirty years her junior.

The old woman had simply felt, deep inside, that this course was the right one to take.

Now she was regretting that decision.

Baba Rana was used to walking everywhere, but a full day's trek over open countryside had taken a terrible toll. Her back and legs throbbed after hours marching across uneven terrain, climbing dykes, and slogging up and down hills. By the time darkness fell, the rests she needed to catch her breath and ease the pain in her chest had grown longer and more frequent. A throbbing ache pulsed behind her eyes and she was swept by waves of nausea.

With night approaching, common sense told the old woman to stop, but that would let her granddaughter get further ahead. Instead, she switched on her torch and doggedly kept going, shining the light directly at her feet to stop herself tripping.

Rana had one advantage. She was more familiar with Fife than her granddaughter and had begun following the abandoned railway line to Newburgh much sooner than Mary. The southern part of the line didn't run a straight course but twisted and turned to avoid hills, which was why she was sure her granddaughter wouldn't join it until after it crossed the A91. But the ground where the tracks had been was flat and free of obstacles and the route, by its very nature, avoided steep inclines and cut a swathe through wooded areas. This made using it far swifter and safer than a more direct course, especially in the dark.

Where the line intersected the A91 it went underneath the road. The engineers who had built the thoroughfare had erected a small bridge over the railway, and most commuters who swept across didn't even notice the abandoned tracks beneath them.

Baba Rana heard the commotion on the A91 long before she saw it. Out of the darkness came the sound of revving engines, commands being bellowed, and people crying.

She switched off her torch and walked uncertainly towards the din, a little old lady lost in a great dark gash, invisible to the melee above. Soon she could see soldiers with guns lining the road, waving a slow-moving column of vehicles by.

Baba Rana gave a small cry. Stumbling to the side of the embankment, she sank to her knees, folding herself deeper into the shadows.

She had seen this *before*.

She couldn't remember how or when, but she *had*. Lines of people hounded and herded along a darkened road by uniformed men.

The old woman got up and staggered through the darkness until she was under the bridge. Here the sounds were muffled, but that made them all the more sinister. She placed her palms flat against the crumbling, moss-sodden brickwork and inched her way under the road. She bent low and shuffled forwards, hands on the ground, edging her way through the night. With agonizing slowness she moved further and further from the chaos on the road, hopelessly trying to shut out the furore and the confusion that gripped her.

The shouting rose dramatically and she looked back.

Fifty yards to the right soldiers were running towards a lone figure who was struggling with one of their number. The figure slammed the man in uniform against a car and then struck him. A shot was fired.

The figure grabbed a smaller form, maybe a girl, leaped off the road and disappeared into the darkness. Baba caught a glimpse of a boy silhouetted against the glow in the sky, arms windmilling, racing into the night behind them.

The old woman bit down on translucent white knuckles.

A fight. A man beaten to the ground. Shots being fired. Children running into the darkness.

She had seen this all *before*.

She bit harder, feeling the metallic tang of blood in her mouth. Even the orange glow in the sky was familiar.

She had witnessed a glow like that before.

A fiery halo over a burning town.

Chapter 35

G ordon and Mary inched through the blackness, arms stretched in front of them. The sound of the engines gradually faded away but, after half an hour, they still hadn't found what they were searching for.

'This is hopeless,' Bobby's father's voice cut through the night. 'We couldn't spot a railway line in this darkness if we fell over it.'

He took another tentative step forwards and vanished.

Mary gave a yelp as she was yanked off her feet. The two fugitives tumbled and rolled down a steep embankment, coming to rest against a line of rusted metal. The girl sat up and felt her arms and legs, but she was unscathed.

'You were saying?'

'Hey. I always had a fine sense of direction.' Gordon's pained voice came from somewhere to the left. 'Could we possibly put the torches on now? I think I'm lying in a patch of nettles.'

With their flashlights trained on the railway line they were able to make swift progress. In less than half an hour the embankment levelled out and they could see the remains of the abandoned Pitlour Station silhouetted against the orange glow, tepees of torn-up rusting girders in the background. The station had always been a makeshift affair and all that was left standing were a couple of boarded-up engine sheds. Mary played both torches on the barricaded windows while Gordon tested the nails that held them in place.

'I can prise these off with a branch or something.'

'It's probably safe to light a fire inside. Nobody will see it.' Mary handed a torch to Gordon. 'You get us in and I'll collect some firewood.'

'OK.' The man began looking around for some sort of lever to force off the slats on the windows. 'Hey! Can't you call Bobby on your mobile? I left mine in the house. Just not used to having one, I suppose.'

'I don't own a mobile,' the girl replied awkwardly. 'And I think Bobby left his in the house too.'

'He did? I thought that thing never left his pocket.'

'Yeah. But some idiot told him the police could track mobile phones.'

'I'm surprised he believed them. Not the trusting sort, our Bobby.'

'Maybe he's learning.' Mary sheepishly turned away and began looking for fuel for their fire.

An hour later Gordon had a small fire going in the middle of the shed. Mary watched him from the doorway, which she had unbarred once they got inside. The man hunched over the fledgling flames, blowing on them until they took proper hold on the damp wood. A flickering lambency danced over Gordon's face giving him a devilish countenance. Mary clenched her fists and winced as her fingernails cut into her grazed palms. For the first time it struck home that she was alone in the wilderness with him. The girl remembered how easily and ruthlessly he had battered the soldier to the ground. When he acted like a teenager it was easy to forget just how broad and muscular he was.

And how unstable.

There was a drawn out lupine howl in the distance. Gordon looked round.

'There are *wolves* in Scotland now?'

'No.' Mary felt the hackles rise on her neck. 'It sounded like one though, didn't it?'

She half-heartedly left the doorway and joined Bobby's father. The concrete floor was freezing, so he had unrolled their sleeping bags to sit on. Mary shared out what was left of their food, leaving some for Bobby. Neither dared mention the possibility that he wouldn't turn up to eat it.

'What do you think was happening back there?' Gordon stuffed a chunk of Mars bar into his mouth. 'Why were there sholdiersh on the road? Where'sh everyone going?'

'I haven't got a clue.' Mary glanced through the window at the orange horizon and shuddered. 'I'm probably being stupid but . . . it seemed like . . . '

'What?'

'It was like the end of the world was starting. And everyone was trying to run away from it.'

'Sorry I asked.' Gordon pulled a piece of twig from his jumper and threw it on the fire. The flames were the same colour as the glow in the sky.

They sat in silence for a while, listening to the fire crackling.

'So . . . are you going *out* with my son?'

'Me?' Mary stammered. 'We're just friends. Anyway he's almost a year younger than me.'

'So? My wife was ten years younger than me.' Gordon stoked the small fire. 'You guys seem right for each other.'

Mary considered this for a moment.

'I'm not very pretty.'

'Oh. Is that it? Well, neither am I.' Bobby's father hugged his knees and stared disconsolately into the flames. 'I'm an old man.'

The two of them sat watching the flickering shadows snake around the concrete walls.

'Gordon,' Mary said. 'How did you know your wife was younger than you?'

'Eh? I've no idea.' The man thought for a second. 'But I *do*.'

'I guess you must have really loved her.'

'I can't have if I left her.'

'Maybe it wasn't your fault.'

'That's the problem. I think and think and I can't remember anything. I'm left with what I feel. And I feel that, somehow, *everything's* my fault.' He hit the side of his head with his palm, as if it would shake loose some blocked memory. 'The officer knew exactly who I was. You heard him.'

'I know.'

'Maybe I'm some sort of secret agent! Maybe I have two identities—Gordon Berlin and Dodd Pollen—and I hit my head or something and got them mixed up.'

'You certainly haven't lost your imagination.' Mary slid her rucksack closer and peered inside. 'Here's an even crazier idea. What if Gordon Berlin and Dodd Pollen are different people in the same body.'

'Yeah. *That* makes sense!' Bobby's father slid his own rucksack across and lay back, using it as a pillow. 'You mean, like a split personality?'

'Not exactly.'

'Then what?'

'Forget it.'

'I'm knackered. Not as young as I used to be, you know. Damn! I feel like someone's hammering bloody nails into my brain.' He sighed and closed his eyes. 'I'm just going to rest for a few minutes, and then I have to go and look for Bobby.'

'I'll come with you when you do.'

'Cool. I don't want to go out there on my own.'

Mary sat quietly watching Bobby's father. His breathing slowly became more rhythmic and his clenched fists relaxed. After a few minutes she realized he had fallen asleep.

'Hmmmm. My dad used to do that as well.'

Mary waited until she was sure Gordon was out for the count. Silently she opened her rucksack and took out a stoppered phial of water and a small Bible. Inside the cover was a thin sheaf of hand-written papers. She dug in the bag again and produced the cross from her bedroom wall. The two halves of the broken Jesus had been fastened back on it with Sellotape—a transparent bandage round his bony torso.

'All right. This is the best chance I'm going to get.'

Clutching the Bible, Mary began to read quietly from her notes. The first part was in Latin and she faltered over many of the words. She kissed the cross and placed it on the floor in front of her.

She unstoppered the phial and began to chant.

'By the power of Jesus Christ our Lord, I compel you, demon, to leave the body of this man. By the power of Jesus Christ our Lord, I compel you, demon, to leave the body of this man.'

Gordon gave a low groan, his face twitching.

She repeated the phrase over and over, picking up and kissing the cross each time she finished. Then she shook the phial in Gordon's direction. Some of the water landed on the fire making it hiss and coil away. A few splashes of water landed on the man's heaving chest. Mary held the cross out towards him, the flickering glow of the fire writhing across his sleeping face.

'By the power of Jesus Christ our Lord I compel you, demon, to leave the body of this man!'

Gordon's eyes shot open.

Chapter 36

Bobby crouched at the foot of a tree, listening intently, hearing nothing but the wind weaving through the branches. The gun was still in his hand, cold and heavy, but he knew that he'd got away.

Bobby had found the revolver in the attic, just like Gordon had said before he lost his memory. Bobby had never seen a real gun before and he'd taken it on impulse. He never thought he'd actually fire it, never mind threaten an army officer with the weapon.

He wondered just how much trouble he was in.

Yet he had never felt the way he did now.

At first he had been terrified, fleeing through utter blackness—a reckless dash that bordered on suicidal. He only stopped when he ran full tilt into a wire fence and was catapulted onto his back with a force that nearly knocked him out. After that he had walked briskly but cautiously, arms stretched in front, trying to put as much distance as he could between himself and the soldiers.

It wasn't hard to keep his bearings, for the orange glow

in the sky was like a signpost saying *north*. If he headed diagonally towards it he was bound to come across the abandoned railway line Mary had been talking about. Then all he had to do was follow it to the derelict station and hope his dad would be there.

He guessed it was safe to use his torch, so he switched it on and headed north-east.

At first every unfamiliar sound made him jump. Then he got used to the owl hoots, cracking twigs, and gusts of wind. They simply added mystery to the wonderful silence in the vast black void he was travelling through. He felt like a mythical hero in some giant inverted cavern, perhaps travelling into the land of the dead to rescue his father.

He put the gun back in his bag. He didn't need it. He felt instinctively that nothing could harm him here. The country-side was finest velvet and the stars glittered like a massive chandelier. But the myriad pinpoints of light didn't make him seem insignificant as they always had before. No. This was *his* black world and he was the most important thing in it.

He stopped, threw back his arms and howled like a wolf, listening to his cry echo across the midnight fields.

'All right. That was totally uncalled for.'

But he couldn't stop smiling. He had saved his dad. He had taken on the army and won. He was walking across Fife on his own in the dark to who knew what fate.

He felt *alive*.

Baba Rana scuttled further and further from the A91, kicking out with her boots to propel herself backwards until she was too exhausted to go any further. Whimpering, she pulled a blanket from her backpack and tugged it over her frail body, hoping the thick wool would provide a little warmth and some measure of camouflage. But her mind wouldn't stop churning. Long-forgotten memories were scratching at the edges of her consciousness, just beyond reach. She sensed, somehow, that she was walking into her own past and, though she didn't know why, it was a place she had never wanted to go.

The old woman clutched at her blanket and pulled it over her head. Shaking with fear and cold and misery, she curled into a ball and cried uncontrollably until she finally fell asleep.

WPC Arnold sat on a hard plastic chair in the interview room of Methil Police Headquarters, hands folded across her knees. Policemen, soldiers, and suited civilians hurried past the door in both directions, gloomy expressions plastered across their faces.

The constable had been there for several hours. Nobody had answered her questions. Nobody paid any attention to her. Sitting alone in the drab windowless room she finally had an inkling of how suspects must feel. If she were a criminal, she'd have been willing to confess a long time ago.

WPC Arnold wondered, for the umpteenth time, if she *had* done something wrong. Surely the insubordination she had shown to the Chief Inspector didn't warrant this kind of treatment?

And she was acutely aware that every hour she stayed here, Gordon Berlin and the children were getting further away.

Chapter 37

Gordon's stare froze Mary to the spot. The Bible and cross were still clutched in the girl's hands.

'What are you playing at, you daftie?' Gordon sat up, wiping drops of water from his face. 'You could have just given me a nudge!'

His eyes fell on the Bible.

'What exactly *are* you doing?'

'Please don't hurt me.' Mary raised the cross in defence. 'I was only trying to help.'

'And what's *that* for?' Gordon's mouth twisted in disbelief. 'I'm not bloody Dracula, you know.'

'I don't know *what* to believe.' Mary slid a little further away, still holding the cross in front of her. 'It was like the end of the world back there. Like Revelation in the New Testament. And you seemed to think it was your fault.'

'I don't think I've caused the end of the world!' Bobby's father gave a guarded laugh. 'Who do you think I am? The Antichrist?'

The girl stayed silent. Gordon's eyes widened as comprehension dawned on him.

'You have *got* to be kidding me!'

'I don't think you're the Antichrist. I just . . .' Mary faltered.

'Just *what*?'

'I think you might be possessed,' the teenager blurted out. 'I think Dodd Pollen is real and that, somehow, he's got inside you.'

'You're an idiot.'

'I'm not!' Mary's eyes flashed defiantly. 'I *saw* something in the church at Puddledub! In the confession booth. It sounded like a demon and it warned me to leave Dodd Pollen alone!'

Gordon tried to repress a snigger.

'I'm not making it up!'

'I know you're not.' The man straightened his face and picked guiltily at his jeans. 'I . . . eh . . . was there.'

'What?'

'I was in my house when someone came snooping round the door calling out that she was Mrs Smith from the boarding kennels and did I want to go to the fete next week. So I sneaked out the back and went looking for Bobby.'

'You went to the church?'

'Yeah, but it was empty. Then I heard someone coming up the path, so I hid in the booth thingy. I didn't realize it was you until Bobby turned up.'

Gordon took a deep, theatrical breath and warped his mouth to one side.

'*Dodd Pollen is here to stay,*' he rasped in a low glottal voice. He gave a cough and tapped his chest. 'It's actually my Donald Duck impression, but I'm not very good at it.'

'*You* were the thing in the confession booth?' The girl's voice was flat and hard.

'I was just having you on. I was going to jump out and give you and Bobby an even bigger fright but you both took off.' Gordon spread his hands. 'It was a joke!'

Mary was still glaring at him. The man tried a half-hearted smile.

'All right, settle down. It was a *stupid* joke.'

'What about the dogs?' The girl waved the cross angrily at Bobby's father. The top half of Jesus came loose and dangled on the strip of Sellotape, arms spread wide in protest. 'They went crazy when you were near them. And how did you know the police were coming to Pennywell Cottage before they even got there?'

'I *didn't* know. I was just making sure that crazy woman from the boarding kennel wasn't still hanging around. And the dogs went nuts because I was throwing stones at them.' He rolled his eyes. 'I thought if I got them barking she'd come and see what the noise was about and I could get back in my home.'

Mary flung the cross to the ground and burst into tears.

'Hey! I didn't hurt the dogs.' Bobby's father scooted round the fire. 'I was just annoying them. Honest.'

'It's not that.' Mary wiped angrily at her face. 'I feel so *stupid*! I *wanted* to believe you were possessed. I thought I finally had proof that God and the Devil and all the stuff in the Bible was real.' She let her hands fall and tears slid freely down her cheeks. 'Then I'd know my mum and dad were really in Heaven and I'd see them again someday.'

'Well . . . they might be.' Gordon picked up the figure and tried to fit Jesus back, but the bottom half came off in his hands. 'That's what faith's supposed to be all about, isn't it?'

'I'm *tired* of believing in things. They never turn out to be true.' The teenager shoved the cross angrily back in her bag. 'It's like my gran. She told me all about Romany sixth sense and folk tales and Little People and I tried to believe that too.'

'Maybe she's right.' Gordon dropped the broken Jesus unceremoniously into the dirt. 'She ought to know, if she's a proper Gypsy.'

'But she's not!' Mary sobbed. 'That's what *I* was going to tell Bobby in the confession booth. She admitted to me long ago that she's not Romany at all. She's just a lonely old lady who loves all that kind of stuff. Just like she loves comic books and superheroes.'

'Me too! The *Green Lantern* is my favourite. Not that it matters,' Gordon added quickly.

'I read Tarot and make spells and I try to convince myself I've got second sight, but the truth is I haven't got a drop of Gypsy blood in me.' The girl slammed shut the Bible with a loud whump. 'I'm a complete fake.'

'Hey, none of us can predict the future. That's probably a good thing.' Gordon put his arm round Mary and gave her a hug. 'I bet it would be hellish if we could.'

He patted her head awkwardly and yawned.

'We can't find Bobby in the dark and we *have* to sleep, Mary. I'm totally pooped and you must be too. As soon as it's light we'll go and look for him. I promise.'

'I suppose that makes sense.'

'The Antichrist!' Gordon chuckled, lying down again. 'Ach. I bet I've been called worse.'

But Mary stayed awake until she was sure the man had drifted off. As she put the broken effigy back in her rucksack, she suddenly remembered a line from one of her favourite films: *The Usual Suspects.*

The greatest trick the devil ever pulled was convincing people he didn't exist.

Chapter 38

The door leading to the Methil police station interview room opened and an army sergeant stuck his head in. WPC Arnold was absurdly pleased to see him. Hours of being given the brush-off was making her paranoid.

'You not gone to get a cup of tea yet, darling?' he said. 'Or something to eat?'

'Eh? Nobody told me I could go get anything.'

'Sorry. We've been a bit . . . preoccupied.' The soldier opened the door wider and beckoned. 'Too late now, anyway. *They* want to see you.'

The policewoman stood up, smoothed down her uniform and followed him into the squad room.

It had changed beyond recognition. Tables had been shoved together and an enormous map of Scotland was spread across their surface. Around the makeshift panorama were several police and army officers together with a handful of civilians. She recognized one or two of them as politicians. Chief Inspector Montgomery, standing to one side, nodded curtly at her.

WPC Arnold stared at the wall behind them. Huge aerial photographs were tacked up everywhere. Each picture showed a different stretch of sea and, judging by the angle, they had been taken from a high flying aeroplane.

The policewoman put a hand to her mouth.

Above the churning water the sky was a broiling sheet of fire, flames stretching from one side of the horizon to the other, from the surface of the sea to the uppermost edge of each photograph.

They looked like gigantic snapshots of Hades.

'Quite a sight, isn't it?' A blond man in a suit gave her a weary smile.

'Can you tell these people what you told me earlier?' the Chief Inspector said. 'About a man named Gordon Berlin.'

WPC Arnold pulled herself up to her full height of five feet five.

'We got a call from one of his neighbours this morning. Rana Szeresewska. She claimed that Mr Berlin had suffered some sort of breakdown and lost his memory. She didn't know the reason, but she believed he was walking to Dundee.'

'And this was second-hand information?' A General with shining brass buttons, and an even shinier bald head, put his hands behind his back and glared at her.

'It was. She was told about the situation by Gordon Berlin's fourteen-year-old son, who then went after his father. As far as I know, her granddaughter has also gone to look for him.'

'Could Berlin be faking?' one of the officers asked his companions.

'Why would he? He couldn't have known about the . . . situation this morning,' the man replied. 'And even if he did, why head towards Dundee? That's even more dangerous than where he was living.'

The General raised a hand to silence everyone. 'Did you find any evidence to back up Mrs Szeresewska's claim?'

'I ascertained that camping equipment had been removed from Gordon Berlin's house,' WPC Arnold continued. 'I also found three sets of fresh footprints in the frost, all heading in the same direction. I'm fairly certain that a handgun was removed from the premises.'

'You know Gordon Berlin, I'm told?' The bald General leaned forwards accusingly.

'We met socially a few times.'

'Did he seem stable to you?'

WPC Arnold thought carefully.

'Yes. He did. He was quite charming, in fact.'

'You were unaware he had a history of mental illness?'

'Until a few hours ago, yes.'

'Good work, Constable,' the Chief Inspector said curtly. 'You can go now.'

WPC Arnold hesitated, her eyes flickering round the walls.

'It's the Norway Sea.' The blond man who had smiled before ran a hand through his hair. 'The sky is on fire. It's like Hell burst out of the ocean.'

'That's classified information!' The General turned his

crossfire stare upon the man in the suit. 'You're in enough trouble as it is, mister!'

'Oh, come on! It's hardly a matter of secrecy now. The whole world is going to know about this in a few hours.'

'May I ask a question?' WPC Arnold cut into the argument, eyes straight ahead. The General harrumphed loudly, before accepting that confidentiality had obviously gone out of the window.

'Ask away.'

'What has all this got to do with Gordon Berlin?' The policewoman motioned towards the photographs.

'Well . . . it's most unfortunate that Mr Berlin has lost his memory and gone walkabout.' The General put both hands on his lower back, leaned back and cracked it loudly.

'Because, apparently, he knew this was going to happen.'

Mary woke in the middle of the night, her neck stiff and cold. The fire had almost died and shadows hung like thick drapes round the walls of the shed. Gordon was lying a few feet away, snoring loudly.

She turned over to get more comfortable.

A shadowy figure was sitting beside her holding his hands out to the feeble flames.

'Bobby!'

The boy grinned, teeth white in the darkness.

'I'm all right,' he said gently. 'Just fashionably late, that's all.'

'God, I was scared!'

'Shhh. It's OK.'

'I'm so glad you're safe.' Mary clutched his hand.

'Nobody can hurt me, toots.'

Mary gave a shudder. 'Bobby, nothing is turning out like I thought.'

'Then stop thinking about how it will turn out.' Bobby lay down beside her. 'Let's just get ourselves to Dundee. Maybe my dad's right. Maybe the answer to all this is in Dundee.'

Mary pulled her blanket up so that he could get under it.

'Don't tell me,' she whispered happily. 'You've got a feeling.'

'I have. But it's probably just my body thawing out.'

'You're a pain in the neck, Bobby Berlin.'

'I know. I learned it from my dad.'

And Mary drifted back to sleep with her friend's arm draped across her.

[MONDAY]

Part 4

The Bridge over the River Tay

And I saw as it were a sea of glass mingled with fire.

REVELATION 15:2

Chapter 39

Bobby's father woke with stabbing pains in his lower back and head, vaguely aware of a crackling sound behind him. He was freezing cold, his neck was stiff, and his arms and leg joints were throbbing. He rolled over with a groan, his eyes gummed half shut. A blurry figure was scraping dirt on to the dying fire and patting it down.

'Morning, Dad.'

'Bobby boy!' Gordon's eyes shot open and he pulled himself upright with a flurry of cracking joints. 'You made it!'

'Yeah. And breakfast is coming right up.' His son gave him a wink. 'We've got a third of a Mars bar each.'

'And a pack of chewing gum.' Mary was stretching in the doorway of the engine shed. A weak sun was shining through her hair and the sky outside was cobalt blue. 'It's a lovely morning. If we get going, I bet we'll reach Dundee in a few hours.'

'Then let's do this.' Bobby stood up, put his hands on his hips and looked down at his father. 'We can eat on the move.'

'Aye, all right. But I'm starving and my back is killing me.' His father groaned and rotated his neck. 'If I get my memory back the first thing I'm going to do is buy a steak pie supper and a feather mattress to lie on while I eat it.'

Mary, Bobby, and Bobby's father were making good progress, despite Gordon constantly grumbling about the pain in his knees.

'So where did the gun come from?' Mary said as they marched towards the crest of yet another hill. 'And you're a moron for waving it around, by the way.'

'Why thank you,' Bobby replied caustically. 'I believe it came from a car boot sale.'

'Oh yes, the gun,' Gordon chimed in. 'I better take that.'

'What? Why?'

'Because you're only fourteen. You could have got yourself killed last night.'

'Yeah? And you *think* you're a kid too. The gun's not any safer with you than it is with me.'

'Hey! Less of the cheek.' Gordon scowled, holding a hand to his aching neck. 'I'm still your dad, remember?'

'And I saved your butt. Remember?' After the escapades of the night before, Bobby was filled with a new-found confidence.

'Ach, just give me the bloody thing,' his father said, holding out his hand.

Bobby held back. He and Gordon had been getting along well but he hadn't forgotten the outburst back at the house, or at the roadside. Besides, if they ran into more soldiers he really didn't want his father to be armed.

'I said, give me the *gun*,' his father repeated, taking Bobby's hesitation as a sign of refusal.

'No.' Bobby took a step back. 'I don't think it's a good idea for you to have it.'

'Since when did you do the thinking?' Gordon's face twitched. 'I'm three times your size, pal. I could *take* the bloody thing if I wanted.'

'Listen to yourself.' Bobby retreated a few feet, stumbling across the pitted earth. 'You can't control your temper. I don't want you shooting the next policeman you see.'

'Don't you sass me!' His father moved forwards. 'Give it here, right now!'

Bobby skipped to one side and his father stumbled and fell flat on his face. Despite himself, Bobby gave a snort of laughter.

Gordon raised his head. He had a raw scrape across his forehead where it had impacted with the ground and his nose was streaked with dirt. His hands curled into fists, one of them closing round a stout branch that was lying next to him. The man's eyes had narrowed to pinpoints.

'Dad?'

'I've had just about enough of this crap,' Gordon hissed. 'First you almost get us caught on that road, then you go waltzing off leaving me and Mary behind.'

'Put that down, Dad.' Bobby suddenly didn't think it wise to mention that it was Gordon who had deserted *him*. 'I'm sorry.'

213

'You going to make me?' Gordon hefted the branch from hand to hand. 'Not so bloody tough now are you?'

'Mr Berlin, what are you doing?' Mary joined in.

'You shut it, an' all!' Gordon swung the branch round. 'I don't need *you* ganging up on me.'

'Who's ganging up? We've been trying to help you!'

'Trying to help me? By waving a bloody Bible in my face!'

'I explained that!'

'No. You were trying to get *rid* of me!' Gordon raised the branch above his head. 'I see it now! You were trying to *stop* me!'

He jabbed the branch at Mary and she leapt back, losing her balance and landing on her back. Gordon gave a sinister chuckle and moved towards her.

'Stop right there, Dodd.'

The man whirled round.

Bobby was pointing the revolver at him.

'Put down the branch.'

'Or what?' Gordon crouched in a defensive stance, circling his son. He tossed the makeshift weapon from hand to hand like some scruffy martial arts expert. 'You better drop that gun or you'll be sorry you ever met me.'

'What's got into you?' his son stammered.

'You put that gun down or I swear you'll get a broken neck.' Gordon's lips curled into a manic grimace. 'I'll batter the living daylights out of you!'

'You're cracking up, Dad. Please don't do this.' Bobby took another step back, the gun trembling in his hand. His father feinted to the left, eyes filled with evil glee.

Bobby dropped the gun and stepped away. Gordon pounced, scooping up the weapon.

'Now, *that* was the stupidest thing you've ever done,' he sneered, pointing the weapon at his son. 'What you going to do now, hero?'

'Dad?'

'Don't dad me!' Gordon cocked the revolver. 'I told you! My name is Dodd Pollen.'

Mary scrambled to her feet, took a deep breath and stepped between them.

'Get out of the way!' Bobby shouted. 'Mary! He's crazy!'

Gordon Berlin's arm wavered. The gun was only inches away from Mary's face.

'Yeah. Get out of the way, girlie,' he mocked.

'I've got faith in you, Mr Berlin.' Mary stepped towards the man, so that the barrel touched her temple. 'I have *faith* in *you*.'

Gordon's cheek began to twitch. Mary didn't move.

With a shuddering intake of breath, Gordon lowered the weapon.

'I just want a bit of respect from Wonder Boy here,' he sulked, his fury evaporating as quickly as it had sparked up. 'You can see that, can't you? If he was always this rude to me, no wonder I didn't like him.'

There was an awkward silence. Bobby glared at the ground.

'Looks like bits of your memory are coming back after all.'

His father dropped the weapon.

'I'm sorry, son,' he said quietly.

'I didn't mean to upset you, honest.' Bobby's voice was strained and quivering.

'No. Shhhhh. Don't apologize.' Gordon put a trembling finger to his lips. 'It's me who should be saying sorry. My God, what did I just *do*?'

'Well, it looked for a bit like you were going to kill me.' His son risked a joke.

'Don't say that!' Gordon flung away the branch. 'Please . . . don't say that.'

'Look. It was a stupid argument and it got out of hand,' Mary cut in, sounding like a disapproving schoolmistress. 'So let's stop fighting and keep going. The Tay should be right over here. We follow it and we'll be at the bridges in a couple of hours.'

Gordon's stubbled chin was quivering as he blinked back tears.

'Oh God,' he whispered. 'I don't know what came over me.'

'Bobby, stick the gun in your bag and give your father a hug.' Mary put her hands on her hips. 'Do it now, and then shake hands.'

And Bobby, white as a sheet, did just that.

Mary nodded and began walking purposefully north— mainly to hide the fact that her legs had turned to jelly.

They walked in strained silence until they came to the top of the hill. Sure enough, the River Tay lay below them, a glistening silver expanse winding its way towards Dundee.

Gordon sidled over to his son.

'Did I have a temper when I was my normal self?'

'No. No, you didn't.'

His father held out one calloused hand. It was shaking like a leaf.

'I can hardly keep my emotions in check,' he said wretchedly. 'I feel like crying, then laughing, then hitting someone. I feel like I'm fighting a war inside myself.'

'You just have to hang on a little longer, Dad.'

'I'm trying.' Gordon glanced round to make sure Mary couldn't hear them. 'Listen. You keep that gun away from me.'

'I won't use it again, don't worry.'

'No, you don't understand. You keep the gun *away* from me.'

Bobby could see a knot of muscle jumping where the man's jaw met his ear.

'And if I act like that again? Next time, you *use* it.'

Chapter 40

The trio skirted Newburgh, staying up on nearby Ormiston Hill. That way they could keep an eye on the village without having to actually go into it.

'We'll save a ton of time if we follow the river road.' Mary pointed to the country lane that led out of Newburgh. 'There's a couple more villages and a few scattered houses on the way but I've got a horrible feeling we won't meet anyone.'

'There's no cars down there.' Bobby studied the village. 'Not even parked ones. And no smoke coming from the chimneys.'

'That's what I mean. The whole area's deserted.' Mary sounded resigned rather than uneasy about the fact. Two days of constant walking, little food or proper sleep, and the constant tension generated by Gordon's condition had begun to unravel her. Her hair was lank and greasy and there were dark circles under her eyes.

'I think we should be trying to *find* people rather than avoiding them. We need to know what's going on around here.'

'*Dundee* can't be empty,' Gordon objected. 'There's three hundred thousand people living there.' He started down the hill and Bobby noticed that he had begun to limp. He caught up with his father.

'Dad, something truly odd is going on and we don't have a clue what it is.'

'All right.' Gordon jutted out his chin to show his displeasure. 'If we spot anybody on the road, we'll ask them what's up. But we see the police or army and we hide, OK?'

His companions were too shattered to argue. Besides, there was nowhere else to go.

But after an hour on the road they hadn't met a living soul. They passed through the hamlets of Ballinbreigh, Fliskmillan, and Hazelton Walls. Each were empty. There were no cars and no people. The shops were locked and shuttered.

At first they approached the villages warily, but it soon became apparent that they were utterly alone. Even Gordon's fear of being accosted gave way to curiosity. He allowed Mary and Bobby to peer in some windows but there were no lights, televisions, or computers on in any of the houses. He even knocked on a door himself then hid behind a bin. Nobody answered.

'This is enough to make *anyone* paranoid,' he stammered, his face slicked with sweat. He ran a hand over his greying jaw, glancing around like an escaped convict.

Bobby watched him uneasily. He and Mary were tense and exhausted but Gordon Berlin was falling apart in front of their eyes.

Eventually they reached Balmerino, one of the last

habitations before the Tay railway bridge. For the first time they could see the thin silhouette crossing the sparkling river. The road bridge, a couple of miles further on, was still out of sight.

'It's not just me, is it? This is really happening.' Gordon flopped down on a bench in the abandoned village square and mopped his face with his T-shirt. 'It's like some kind of fairy tale gone wrong.'

'No point in turning back now.' Mary sank down beside him and took off her bag. 'And I'm dumping this rucksack. There's nothing much in it except my cross, which obviously has no effect on you.'

'You back on this possession crap again?'

'What am I supposed to think?' Mary snapped, too beaten to be afraid. 'You almost killed your own son.'

'Aw, shut it. Where's he gone anyway?'

As Gordon spoke, Bobby came running past, his head down and a determined expression on his face.

'What are you *doing*?' his father called.

The teenager sprinted across the square towards the grocery store on the corner, speeding up as he reached the building. Mary clapped her hands to her face.

Bobby hit the shop door with his shoulder and it burst open with a sickening crunch. He vanished into the dark interior, yelping in pain. Gordon jumped to his feet and looked around in panic.

'What the bloody hell is he playing at?'

Bobby appeared triumphantly in the doorway, holding his arm.

'I'm all right!' he grinned through clenched teeth. 'Now, who wants a sandwich and a Coke? Lunch is on me.'

Baba Rana had jettisoned her own rucksack miles back. Then her heavy coat. The ribbon that held her hair in place was coming loose and wisps of white hair were stuck to her lined, perspiring face.

Like Mary, Gordon, and Bobby, she had passed village after village, all bereft of people. It all seemed so familiar. The empty houses. Deserted towns.

She was approaching the village square in Balmerino when she heard raised voices and a crash. She quickly turned into a side road and avoided the town centre. Something, some buried memory, made her shy away from any loud noises.

Baba Rana desperately wanted to rest but knew she was running out of time. Half an hour away was the Tay railway bridge and, two miles beyond that, the road bridge. That bridge had a pedestrian walkway. That was where her granddaughter would have to cross if she wanted to reach Dundee.

She pulled her cigarette packet from her pocket, but it was empty. Rubbing red rimmed eyes, the old woman threw it away and left Balmerino, heading east.

Chapter 41

WPC Arnold sprawled across two chairs, drifting in and out of sleep. Her cap had fallen to the floor, blonde hair spread across her face in a disordered veil.

She felt a nudge in her side and opened her eyes. A polystyrene cup hung in front of her face. The blond man who had spoken to her in the operations room was crouched beside the chairs, a coffee in each hand. His suit was wrinkled, his tie squint, and his eyes bleary. Behind him stood a pilot in a green flight suit.

'You'll have to wake up,' the man said. 'The command centre is relocating to Newburgh, further inland. The police have orders to head west to safety and let the army deal with the last of the evacuation.'

WPC Arnold sat up and gratefully accepted the cup. She yawned, stretched, and took a slurp of the black liquid. The man rose to leave.

'I'm sorry, I didn't catch your name.'

'Ashley Gosh.'

'May I ask you a question, Mr Gosh?'

'Call me Ashley.'

'*What* evacuation?'

'I assumed you had been briefed.' Ashley looked surprised.

'Briefed? I've hardly been tolerated.'

'The stuff that's burning is methane. Natural gas. First warning we got that there was a huge methane release in the North Sea was when ships began sinking.'

'Sinking?'

'Methane gas smells like sulphur and is incredibly inflammable. It's also much lighter than water. Any boat passing over an underwater methane deposit suddenly has nothing to float on. It goes straight down.' Ashley Gosh fanned his coffee with a trembling hand. 'Then a whole oil rig vanished. That's when we knew the methane escape had to be gigantic.'

'And now it's been ignited?'

'Yup. Probably struck by lightning. And we have reliable evidence that this release of burning gas will destabilize an underwater mountain range in the Norway Sea, called Storegga, and cause it to collapse. It'll generate a tidal wave that will reach the east coast of Scotland.

'Generate a *what*?'

'A tidal wave. A tsunami.'

As a policewoman, WPC Arnold's first instinct was to gather as much information as possible.

'How big a tidal wave?'

'We don't know for sure. The last time Storegga slid was

several thousand years ago, but we can tell the size of that tsunami by the alluvial deposits it left behind.'

WPC Arnold waited.

'It was thirty metres high when it hit the Scottish coast.'

The policewoman blanched.

'Of course, there were very few people living there at that time. But now there are three major cities on the east coast—Edinburgh, Aberdeen, and Dundee. Hence the evacuation.'

'I'm not an expert in geology.' The policewoman put down the cup and stretched her back. 'But I've heard about this before.'

'Sorry?'

'I used to sit in the pub with your friend and mine, Gordon Berlin. When he got drunk he talked about that sort of thing. Seemed very knowledgeable on the subject. Of course I didn't think much about it at the time. I do now.'

Ashley glanced up and down the corridor. People were hurrying back and forth but nobody was paying much attention to them.

'Jensen.' He turned to the man in the flight suit. 'Could you fetch us some coffee?'

'You have one in your hand,' the man replied, staring ahead.

'Then get one for my other hand.'

Jensen pursed his lips and marched off down the corridor. Ashley leaned in close.

'You have the beat on the Fife coast?'

'I do.'

'I've got a house there.' Ashley slid down, his back against the wall. 'I used to run the ethylene plant near Inverkeithing for Secron Oil. I was very ambitious in those days.'

WPC Arnold couldn't see what that had to do with anything, but she let the man talk. As a policewoman, she instinctively knew when a person wanted to get something off their chest.

'It was a mess when I took over. Poor production levels. Couldn't compete. I turned it around.'

WPC Arnold would have expected most men to take pride in that statement. But Gosh sounded sickened.

'I fired slackers. Worked others to the bone. Cut corners. Did so well, Secron promoted me to head a new venture called the Lazarus Project.'

'Go on.'

'A few years ago, Secron's exploration teams discovered huge underwater deposits of methane hydrate—frozen gas, if you like—under the sea bed, in the area of the Norway Sea known as Ormen Lange. The Lazarus Project was an attempt to revitalize the depleted gas reserves in the North Sea by developing technology that would let us get at those enormous frozen gas fields.'

WPC Arnold leaned forward, listening intently.

'But there was a problem. Ormen Lange is very close to the edge of the Storegga underwater mountain range. One or two environmental groups were worried that drilling there might cause that underwater shelf to destabilize.'

'Don't tell me you went ahead?'

'Our experts did exhaustive research into that possibility and assured us it couldn't happen.' Ashley took a sip of his own coffee, the steam hiding his eyes. 'Government researchers came to the same conclusion, so yes, drilling commenced a couple of months ago.'

Ashley loosened his tie and scratched his chest.

'There was only one dissenter, a marine geologist working for Secron on the drilling rig itself. His name was Gordon Berlin.'

WPC Arnold closed her eyes.

'He predicted a scenario that just seemed too far-fetched to be plausible. He claimed drilling would cause large chunks of the frozen methane hydrate under the area of Orman Lange to break up and melt. According to his calculations, if this methane were to ignite, the pressure change would trigger another slide on the Storegga fault. He was certain this slide would occur within twenty-four hours of any conflagration.'

'And nobody listened to him?' WPC Arnold spat incredulously.

'Nobody got the chance,' Ashley said miserably. 'Secron discovered that Mr Berlin had once been diagnosed with a condition known as Narcissism. He thought he was smarter than everyone else. He couldn't accept the possibility that he might be wrong.'

Ashley Gosh sipped his coffee, squinting through the steam.

'It was the end of him. His credibility was lost.'

'Problem being, he was right.'

'He was a lone dissenter and, considering his past, Secron made him a very generous offer. If he resigned and promised not to discuss his theory, he would be offered a large cash settlement. He wasn't a stupid man. He knew the alternative—that he'd be fired and have his medical history . . . eh . . . *accidentally* leaked to the press. Not much of a choice for a man who had just discovered his ex-wife was dead and he had a son to look after.'

'Jeez! Knowing what he knew, I'm surprised he didn't go off the deep end sooner!'

'I almost wish he had. His timing couldn't have been worse.' Ashley gave a dry laugh. 'I tried to warn him, you know. Went to his house on Saturday night. But I didn't realize he'd lost his memory and I guess I only made things worse.'

'Do you know where he is now?'

'He was spotted by an army unit in north Fife, but got away from them.' Ashley let his head drop. 'He had those kids with him. He's obviously still heading for Dundee and, as far as I can tell, has no idea what's going on. But the army are evacuating whole cities, Constable. They haven't got the manpower to search for three individuals.'

'That's not fair.'

'I know. But there's not much we can do about it.'

'Oh yeah? Well, *I'll* find him.' WPC Arnold snatched up her hat and slammed it onto her head. 'He's my friend. I know his son.'

'All the roads are clogged. You wouldn't even get close.'

'Then I'll damned well walk. He and the children are doing it.' The policewoman struggled to her feet, massaging her legs. 'He deserves that, at least.'

'Wait . . . wait.' Ashley stood up and put a hand on her shoulder. 'I . . . eh . . . I have a private helicopter on stand-by, waiting to take me to Newburgh.'

'How very nice for you.'

'That's not what I meant. I have an idea.' The man spotted the Chief Inspector approaching down the corridor. Behind him was Jensen, carrying two cups of coffee.

'Excuse me? Inspector?'

'What is it?' The man could barely conceal his distaste at having to talk to a Secron executive.

'If my chopper took WPC Arnold to Wormit police station near the Tay Bridge could you have a police car fuelled up and waiting for her?'

'And why would I do that?'

'She wants a last chance to look for Gordon Berlin. If you agree, you can keep my 'copter to help with the evacuation after you've dropped her off.'

'I'm sorry, sir, but you can't do that.' Jensen broke in, still holding the steaming cups. 'It's not your helicopter. It's the property of Secron Oil.'

'Which has been placed at my disposal.'

'With all due respect, sir.' Jensen sounded anything but respectful. 'We are to pick up an important cargo at Newburgh and move it to safety. Those orders come from the chairwoman herself.'

'There's been a change of plan.'

'I received these orders directly from the chairwoman,' Jensen insisted.

'I'm here. She's not. You're fired.' Ashley Gosh raised an eyebrow at the Chief Inspector. 'Do we have a deal?'

'And you *want* to go?' the Chief Inspector said to WPC Arnold.

'I'll get out at the first sign of trouble.'

'I can't let you do that.' Jensen threw the coffee in the bin and unclipped a satellite phone from his belt. 'I need to talk to my boss.'

'You keep quiet before I throw you in a cell for obstructing the police.' The Chief Inspector pulled the device out of Jensen's hand and smashed it against the wall. 'A cell that may well be underwater in a few hours.'

He turned to Ashley Gosh.

'I appreciate you telling us about Gordon Berlin's research,' he said. 'But you know this doesn't let you off the hook.'

'I know.'

'Be ready in ten minutes, Constable. I'll find you a different pilot.' The Inspector patted the woman on the shoulder and carried on up the corridor. Jensen followed him, still protesting. Ashley Gosh got up to leave.

'Mr Gosh.' WPC Arnold tilted her cap back. 'How did Secron Oil know about Gordon Berlin's medical problem? I'm sure he didn't exactly advertise the fact.'

'You're very good at what you do, aren't you?' Ashley permitted himself a small smile. 'As I said, I live near the ethylene plant. It's a pretty close-knit community in that area and I got to know the people there. Including a woman named Alison Berlin.'

His mouth turned down at the corners.

'One night, over a few drinks, I asked why her husband had left her and she told me about his . . . condition.'

'And you informed your bosses at Secron Oil.'

'I did.'

WPC Arnold pushed blonde locks away from her face.

'When this is over, you *know* I'll have to come after you.'

'I won't be very hard to find.' Ashley took off his jacket and slung it resignedly over his shoulder.

'I'm going home.'

Chapter 42

The North Sea
30 Miles off the Coast of Scotland

Eddie Hall sat on the deck of the *Lillian Gish* playing his tin whistle. He was still astonished by the clarity and serenity of its timbre, but even the lilting sound couldn't lift his spirits. The sun was beginning to rise, washing away the sickly glow that had flickered faintly behind them through the hours of darkness.

Eddie hadn't slept for most of the night. If he was honest with himself, he'd been too afraid. Instead he had sat in the wheelhouse with the earpiece of the communication tube on the navigation table beside him. He could hear the sporadic clink of bottle on glass coming from the captain's cabin as the skipper drank himself into a stupor.

Then Eddie had lashed the wheel, gone below deck, found Lasse Salvesson's private trunk and searched through it. The first mate, he knew, owned a little wireless on which he listened to Norwegian radio when the *Lillian Gish* was at sea. Eddie had found it, crept up on deck, and tuned in to the shipping channel.

Something was wrong. He felt it in his soul.

And something *was* very wrong.

WPC Arnold stood in the car park of Wormit police station, just out of range of the whipping wind created by the rotating blades of the helicopter. On either side the twin ribbons of the Tay road and railway bridges stretched across the river to Dundee.

The Chief Inspector shook her hand, the bottom of his jacket flapping backwards and forwards.

'Everyone else is gone, but there's one police car at the back with a tank full of petrol,' he shouted. 'Dundee has been evacuated and so has the south bank of the Tay, all the way up to Newburgh. There's two platoons of soldiers left in the city to make sure there are no looters but they'll be leaving on troop trains soon.'

'Thank you, sir, I'll take it from here,' WPC Arnold yelled back.

'Have this.' He handed her a field radio. 'I'll get someone to call you if a slide begins at Storegga. A tidal wave can travel at five hundred miles an hour, you know.' He tapped his watch to emphasize the point he was making. 'When that happens it will only take ninety minutes before it hits this area.'

'I understand.' WPC Arnold glanced around, impatient to begin her search.

'I mean it!' Chief Inspector Montgomery bent low so that his words wouldn't be lost in the deafening whirr of rotor blades. 'The two troop trains still in Dundee will carry the last of the soldiers out. When you see them crossing the railway bridge you'll know you've run out of time. All the roads in this area are empty now, so get in the car and drive like hell.'

He gripped the woman by the shoulder.

'Good luck, Constable . . . eh . . . just what is your first name?'

'Joanne, sir.'

'Joanne.' The Chief Inspector shook her hand. 'I'll have that put on your medal for bravery. When we next meet, I hope to be pinning it on you.'

'Let's just hope you don't end up putting it on my tombstone.'

Captain Morrison came on deck, eyes bleary, hair and beard matted. He sniffed the air and was seized by a fit of coughing that doubled him over. He shook his hoary head like a bear coming out of hibernation, spat a wad of phlegm onto the deck and wiped his mouth with the sleeve of his greatcoat.

'What's our position and heading, sailor?'

'About twenty miles east of Wick, Skipper.' Eddie tucked the flute into his waistband. 'We're locked on a south-easterly course.'

'I need some coffee.' The captain lurched towards the wheelhouse. 'My tongue feels like a mohair jumper that's been tumble dried. What time do you estimate we'll reach Dundee?'

'Not too long.' Eddie tried to keep his voice as calm as possible. 'Unless the tidal wave gets there first.'

Captain Morrison's back stiffened and he slowly turned around. He noticed the tiny radio perched on the wooden bench beside the sailor.

'Makes for interesting listening, does it?' He leaned against the cabin wall. 'Whatever you heard, it's just speculation.'

'It's a nationwide alert, Skipper.' Eddie stood up, legs apart and hands dangling by his side. He had hidden a marlinspike behind the bench where he'd been sitting, just in case. It was used for hooking and stunning large fish but would work just as well on the captain. 'The Met Office says that huge methane deposits are on fire in the North Sea. They claim it will cause a tsunami that'll wipe out the east coast of Scotland.'

'They've been wrong plenty of times before.' The skipper appeared unruffled. 'It's not proof of anything.'

'And what would proof be?' Eddie spluttered. 'The *Lillian Gish* ending up in the top of a tree?'

'And just what advice *did* the Met Office give to ships?'

'To stay at sea. A tidal wave is only dangerous when it reaches land and gathers height. In the open ocean we'll barely feel it passing under us.'

'I know how the tides work, boy. Did they give any other recommendations?'

Eddie hesitated. 'As an alternative, they suggested sailing into an estuary and getting as far up river as possible.'

'And that's exactly what we're going to do.' Another

bout of coughing racked Captain Morrison. He spat again and took in a gulp of sea air. 'We'll head into the Firth of Tay and up the river. By the time the *Lillian Gish* reaches Newburgh we'll be further inland than any wave can reach.'

'The Firth of Tay is too far away!' Eddie refused to back down. 'We could head out to deep ocean and be safe.'

'Sailor, what we're carrying could put us in jail for years.' The skipper pressed thumbs into his eyes and shook his head to clear it. 'We need to get *rid* of this cargo and the only place we can do it is Newburgh.'

'We could dump it over the side.'

'That's out of the question.'

'Why? What exactly *is* our cargo, Skipper?'

Captain Morrison clumped over. Eddie's hand reached behind him, just in case, but the bearded man snorted humourlessly.

'I'm not going to harm you.' He plonked himself down beside the sailor. 'I can't operate the damned ship myself, and you know it.'

'What are we carrying?' Eddie repeated.

'Treasure.'

'Skipper, this is a fishing trawler, not the damned *Jolly Roger*!'

'Be that as it may, treasure is what we're carrying.' Captain Morrison gave a bitter smile. 'During World War Two the Waffen SS had a branch called the Ancestral Heritage Research and Teaching Society. They were obsessed with the occult and scoured the globe for artefacts they believed had supernatural significance. Or were just worth a lot of money.' He wiped at his mouth again. 'Terrible, I know, but worth a fortune on the black market. Their plunder is what we have on board.'

'Is it worth dying for?' Eddie thought of Lasse Salvesson. 'Our share is only a few thousand each.'

'You don't understand. Historically, these artefacts are priceless.' The captain scratched his beard awkwardly. 'I sort of lied about the size of our share.'

Eddie cocked his head. 'How big a lie?'

'Our cut is £500,000.'

Eddie Hall's jaw dropped.

'You cheap conniving . . . ! You said I was getting five thousand for the whole trip.'

'You were.' Captain Morrison shrugged nonchalantly. 'But circumstances have changed somewhat. Get us to Newburgh and I'll split it with you. £250,000 to be exact. Still want to dump the cargo over the side?'

'I'm reconsidering, it has to be said.'

'This old girl can make it.' Morrison patted the rail of his ship. 'In a way, the disaster has worked in our favour. The coastguard, the army, the police, they'll be dealing with a massive evacuation. If we reach Newburgh, they won't have the time or the inclination to look twice at the *Lillian Gish*.'

Eddie couldn't help himself.

'Things didn't work out all right for Lasse Salvesson.'

The light seemed to drain from Captain Morrison's eyes.

'I sailed with the first mate for years,' he said. 'He was a dour man, objectionable even, but then so am I. We never had an argument before. Not one.'

He leant back against the wheel and stared into the sky, ashamed to look at his crewmate. 'He tried to use the radio to get more information about what was happening. Against my orders. That's mutiny, in my book.'

'No it's not, Skipper. It's common sense.'

'I tried to stop him and the set landed on the floor and broke. Salvesson stormed out and I went after him. I was drunk and I was mad.' Captain Morrison gave a hiccup. 'I caught up with him by the stern and grabbed him and he tried to pull free.'

'You pushed him *overboard*?'

'I did not! I slipped and lost my balance and it looked like I was going over the side. The first mate reached out to pull me back and I lashed out at him and hit my head on the bulwark.' A broken, bitter exhalation escaped the big man's glistening lips. 'When I woke he was gone. I circled for half an hour but I couldn't see him. Not that it would have mattered. Nobody could last more than a few minutes in that water without a lifebelt.'

The captain looked with undisguised hate at the flute tucked into Eddie's belt.

'Salvesson was right, you know. This cargo is cursed. I should have listened to him.'

'So what do we do now?'

'We break the curse, lad. Only way I can think to do that is deliver the cargo and hope we never see it again.'

Eddie looked fearfully across the ocean. But it was flat and smooth as marble.

'Aye aye, Skipper,' he said sadly.

'Me and Lasse? We had no family, neither of us. He was a plain man and not much fun but we'd sailed together for . . . I forget how many years. And he died saving my life.'

Tears began to trickle down Captain Morrison's cheeks.

'I killed my best friend.'

WPC Arnold parked her car next to the Tay road bridge and got out, a pair of binoculars round her neck. She remembered Gordon Berlin saying that one of the two bridges was the longest in the world when it was built, but she couldn't recall which. She focused the binoculars on the structure but there was nobody on the pedestrian walkway. Perhaps Gordon and the children had already crossed. If they had, there was no way she would find them in the deserted city. Best to stay here and hope they would show up on the Fife side.

The field radio crackled and she picked it up.

'This is Sergeant Cooper, second Battalion of the Black Watch. Over.'

'WPC Arnold here.'

'It's happened, Constable.' The interference couldn't mask the shock and disbelief in the soldier's voice. 'There's been a massive slide at Storegga and a tsunami is heading towards the coast of Scotland. You need to get out of there pronto.'

WPC Arnold's heart lurched.

'I've got an hour and a half before it hits, Sergeant.'

'With all due respect, ma'am,' Cooper replied firmly. 'We don't know how far inland the wave will reach. I strongly suggest you head for higher ground right now.'

'Understood. I'm going to make one more circuit of the area. If I don't find anyone, I'll get the hell out.'

'I've too much to do to argue with you. Good luck, Constable. Please don't get a flat tyre.'

WPC Arnold smiled, despite herself.

'I'll drive on the rims if I have to. Over and out.'

Eddie Hall stuck his head into the wheelhouse of the *Lillian Gish*. He was in a state of high agitation.

'The Storegga slide has started! How long will it take the wave to reach us?'

'What does the Met Office say?' Captain Morrison was crouched over the wheel, willing the ship to go faster.

'I can't tell! The reception is all garbled on this piece of . . .'

'Look! We're only fifteen miles from Dundee.' The captain waved his hand at the navigation instruments. 'Go sit on deck and play your damned flute or something. Storegga is almost a thousand miles away. We'll be out of danger in a couple of hours.'

Chapter 42

Baba Rana finally reached the Tay railway bridge and sat down to rest. The iron girders towered over her and she lay back on the damp grass, staring up through thick black triangles at the heavy grey sky. She closed her eyes for a second and almost nodded off.

She heard a click-clack noise above. The woman gave a start and opened her eyes.

A troop train was crossing the bridge, coming from the direction of Dundee. It was dull grey and packed with soldiers. As it passed overhead she could see anxious faces staring out of the windows.

She suddenly remembered another train filled with terrified troops—only these soldiers had different uniforms.

She caught a movement out of the corner of her eye and twisted round.

The boy from the ethylene plant was heading down the coast road in the direction of the road bridge. He glanced back at the train, gave a frightened skip and increased his speed. The woman struggled to her feet.

'Gorgio!' she cried out. 'Wait! It's me. It's Rana!'

Wait. I just called his name! she thought. *How do I know his name?*

For the strange run, the shock of dark hair, even the slope of the boy's back were suddenly all too familiar. And not just from a few days ago.

'Gorgio! Wait for me! Please!'

Baba Rana staggered up the riverbank and on to the road as quickly as her aching legs could carry her. A stabbing pain shot through her upper body, bringing her to a gasping halt. Clutching her chest, she sank to her knees, her head spinning.

The boy was getting further and further away. Taking a deep breath, Rana rose to her feet and forced herself to hobble after him, just as she had so many years ago.

This time she would not let Gorgio get away.

This time she would catch up with her brother.

WPC Arnold shot along the shoreline and skidded to a halt beside the railway bridge. This structure didn't have a walkway and looked pretty unsafe to cross on foot, even without trains running. Still, she wanted to be sure. She trained her binoculars on the girdered giant but there was no sign of life. An icy wind had sprung up and she buttoned her police jacket.

'I'll check the road bridge once more. One more check. I've got time.'

* * *

Lying flat on the embankment that sloped up to the bridge, Gordon watched the Panda rocket away.

'Bloody women drivers,' he muttered.

'That's her all right.' Bobby propped himself on one elbow. 'The same policewoman you used to go drinking with.'

'I can't believe the cops are still looking for me. Doesn't that woman ever give up?'

'She's very pretty.' Mary rolled over on her back. 'We should have talked to her.'

'I'm not particularly talkative with handcuffs on,' Bobby's father retorted. 'And we're *so* close to Dundee.'

'So what do we do now?'

'She's probably setting up bear traps at the road bridge.' Gordon looked longingly at the city across the water. It was too far to be sure, but there seemed to be no sign of life there either. 'We'll have to cross this one.'

'The railway bridge? What if a train comes?'

'Let's face it.' Gordon gave an embittered snort. 'There's nobody for miles except us and that bloodhound in uniform. I don't think there's going to be any trains crossing.'

'Let's walk fast, just in case. Get this done.' Bobby scrambled up the embankment and onto the railway track. With a fretful glance at his father he turned and started off towards Dundee. Gordon gave a shrug and followed him. Mary hesitated at the top, stepping onto the tracks and back off again. Bobby looked back at his nervous friend.

'I got a feeling, Bobby.'

'You want to stay here?'

Mary thought for a moment.

'Not on my own I don't.'

And she hopped onto the bridge and ran after her companions.

WPC Arnold slowed to a halt beside the road bridge and got out of the car.

'Well, I'll be damned . . . '

There was an old woman sitting on a bench overlooking the river. The constable slammed the car door and hurried over to her. As she got closer she realized who it was.

'What on earth are you doing here?' she asked, sitting down beside Baba Rana. The woman looked at the end of her tether, frail and shivering in the wintry breeze. Her head was bare, apart from a red ribbon hanging limply from her ponytail.

'I walked,' she said listlessly. 'I was following my granddaughter.'

'Have you seen any sign of her? Or Bobby and Gordon Berlin?'

'No.' Baba Rana stared out over the water. 'But I *am* waiting for a sign.'

'You stay here and you'll get a lot more than a sign.' WPC Arnold looked at her watch. 'We need to leave this place right away.'

'I have a confession to make.'

'Best save it for another time.'

'When I was a little girl, my family were hunted by the

Nazis. We were Gypsies, you see. Undesirables. But that wasn't really why they were after us.'

'I'm sure this is an interesting story, ma'am.' WPC Arnold held up her hand. 'But it really will have to wait.'

'I *have* waited. I've waited almost seventy years to remember.' The woman clutched angrily at WPC Arnold's sleeve. 'Finally, I *do*. I *must* tell someone. I haven't any time left.'

The constable looked around hopefully. Perhaps Gordon and the children were just over the next hill. After all, if an old woman could make it here . . .

'Go on, then. But make it quick.'

'It was nineteen forty-five. My people, a Romany group of about twenty, were trying to reach the British and American lines. The German defences were crumbling, but one SS group had chased us for months. The *Ahnenerbe Forschungs und Lehrgemeinschaft*, they were called—the Ancestral Heritage Research and Teaching Society.'

'Doesn't sound like a bunch of teachers to me. And I went to a pretty tough comprehensive.'

'They were an SS group. Thieves and plunderers. We must have had something they wanted very badly. One night they finally found us. The men tried to fight their way out and my father told my brother and me to run for the woods.'

A tear slid down Baba Rana's wrinkled cheek.

'He told us that, if we were caught, we were to say that we were both good German children. That the Gypsies had kidnapped us. He told us to deny who we were. My brother

Gorgio wouldn't hear of it, but my father made him swear a solemn oath. He handed us his most prized possessions—a flute that had been in his family for generations and a ribbon that belonged to my mother. That's when I knew we would never see him again.'

WPC Arnold stood up and looked around again. Still no sign of Gordon and the children.

'We didn't get very far before the Germans captured us. We told our story to the SS officer, as my father had instructed, but he didn't believe it. We were put on a train, the carriages filled with broken, beaten people, and taken many miles to a strange place. My brother told me it was called *Auschweiken*. Auschwitz.'

The policewoman slowly sat down, listening properly for the first time.

'It had sheds and huge chimneys and smelt of sulphur and gas. Just like the ethylene plant next to where I live.' The woman clasped her hands together, thinking of her sketch pad. 'All my life I thought I had drawn something from the future, when I was really drawing something from the past.'

'I'm not sure I understand.' WPC Arnold reached out and took the woman's hand. 'But you really will have to finish this story later.'

'My brother knew why we hadn't been believed.' The old woman ignored the interruption. 'I had fair hair and blue eyes and could pass as Germanic, but he . . . he had thick black hair and his skin was olive. So . . . when we got off the train he told the officers there a different story.'

Baba Rana's face crumpled.

'He told them that only *I* had been kidnapped. He said that he had grown to love me and that he had to tell the truth, because he couldn't bear to see me killed in a gas chamber. This time they believed him. Even allowed Gorgio to say goodbye.'

The woman gave a choked sob.

'It was bitterly cold. Like today. My brother was older than me but he was a slight boy and very small for his age. I gave him my coat and hat to wear and he fixed the ribbon in my hair and handed me the flute. He said this was part of my Gypsy heritage and more important than I could imagine. That it was the reason the Nazis had chased us for so long. Then he kissed my forehead, put on the coat, and walked away.'

Baba Rana began to cry.

'From the back he looked just like me.'

WPC Arnold swallowed hard.

'There was a troop train leaving Auschwitz,' Rana continued through tears. 'The regular soldiers were fleeing because the Allies were coming. I ran after Gorgio, but, before anyone could stop him, he threw himself under the wheels.'

The constable felt tears well up in her own eyes.

'I'm sorry,' she said. 'I'm really sorry.'

'One officer picked me up and took me to his staff car. Another took away my flute. I couldn't even keep my father's flute!'

Dry sobs racked her feeble body. WPC Arnold took off her police tunic and draped it over the woman's shoulders.

'Here. You're freezing.'

'I blanked all this from my mind!' Baba Rana stammered. 'I couldn't bear to remember what had happened.'

She wiped angrily at her tear-streaked face.

'But that isn't the worst part.'

'It can get *worse*?'

'I told my daughter and my granddaughter that we weren't of real Gypsy blood. That the caravan in the garden was just an old woman's pipe dream. Somewhere deep down, I didn't ever want them to be persecuted for who they were. I fooled them into denying their roots, just like I denied mine.'

The woman looked sorrowfully at WPC Arnold.

'My granddaughter is a real Romany and she doesn't even know it. That's why my brother has come back. He wants me to remember. Wants my granddaughter to know who she really is.'

And you are a delusional old woman, WPC Arnold thought, though it only made her feel more sorry for the confused soul. She rubbed Baba Rana's arms to restore some circulation, took off her hat and placed it on the old woman's uncovered head, tucking wisps of white hair under the peak. It wasn't much protection against the biting cold but it was the best she could do.

'Listen, ma'am. We have to get you out of here before you die of hypothermia.' She put her arm round the old woman. 'Let's go to the car and take you somewhere safe.'

Baba Rana was staring across the river.

'Listen,' she said, a slow smile spreading across her face.

'I don't think there's anything to hear.' WPC Arnold cocked her head just to humour the old lady.

'I can hear my father's flute.'

And there it was. The faint echo of a beautiful melody floating across the silvery expanse. WPC Arnold took a step back, shaking her head. The old woman looked up and patted her companion's arm.

'Do you know what we Gypsies believe? We believe it's unlucky to die at home. That's why Romanies must travel somewhere else when their time has come.'

'Nobody's going to die, ma'am.'

Baba Rana smiled again and got slowly to her feet. Her eyes were unfocused and glassy.

'I'm ready to go now.'

The constable nodded, casting a last surreptitious look over the area. The sun had almost set. It was already too dark to see the railway bridge properly and even the road bridge was beginning to blend into the shadows. She helped Baba Rana into the back seat of the car, got behind the wheel and sped towards higher ground.

Gordon, Mary, and Bobby were nearing the north side of the railway bridge when Bobby's father stopped dead.

'Dad.' Bobby poked him in the arm. 'Could we speed it up a bit? We're on a railway line with nowhere to run if a train comes. Remember?'

Gordon pointed to where the estuary widened and joined the sea.

'What are those?'

Bobby followed his gaze. It was hard to see properly for the sky was rapidly turning to ink.

'Oil derricks,' he said. 'I suppose they towed them down here for repairs. Why?'

His father looked around.

'It happened *here*,' he said. 'Not in Dundee.'

'What. What happened here?'

'Everything.'

'Are you OK, Dad?'

Gordon didn't move.

'Dad?'

Gordon Berlin swallowed hard. Then his eyes rolled up into his head and he slumped onto the track.

WPC Arnold glanced at the speedometer. She was doing ninety miles an hour but there was no traffic on the road and no chance of meeting any, so she pressed down harder on the accelerator.

'There's a range of hills just next to Cupar,' she shouted. 'We can be there in ten minutes. Just have to hope they're high enough. The tidal wave is going to hit the coast any minute.'

There was silence from the rear of the car. A thought struck the constable.

'You do *know* about the tidal wave?'

She looked in the rearview mirror and almost lost control of the car.

Baba Rana's head had fallen back and she was staring sightlessly at the roof.

'You OK, ma'am? Please say something!'

The old woman's head lolled to one side and a lock of white hair slipped from under the police hat.

The policewoman swore loudly and screeched the car to a halt. Lurching over the seat she gripped the old woman's wrist and felt for a pulse.

There was none.

Baba Rana was dead.

'Goddammit!' WPC Arnold jerked away and thumped the seat. Rana slid sideways, head lolling over her bony shoulders.

With the unruly hair drifting down from the hat and the police jacket fastened round her thin body, Baba Rana looked like an ancient version of WPC Arnold. The constable closed her eyes and crossed herself.

Wasn't much of a way for a person to die. All alone in the back of a stranger's car.

'I'll find your granddaughter, madam. I'll tell her what you told me. I promise.'

She let go of Rana's hand, wormed her way back into the driver's seat and grasped the wheel.

'If I actually live through this.'

Then she floored the accelerator.

Chapter 43

Dundee:
5 January 1977

It was Sunday night. The sky was a deepening bruise, turning the shadows below the railway bridge into tar. Gordon Berlin huddled against one of the huge concrete supports breathing as quietly as possible. Behind him he could just make out a line of jagged iron stumps protruding from the moonlit waters of the Tay. They were all that remained of the original bridge, swept away in a storm a century ago, taking the train that had been crossing with it. There had been no survivors.

The boy shivered at the thought of all the angry spirits that might be hanging around this structure.

'Stop acting so soft,' he said to himself. 'You're fourteen, not a ten-year-old girl.'

'Yeah. Stop acting so soft.' A figure appeared round the other side of the support and the boy almost fell over.

'Is that you, Dodd?'

'Nah, it's the Yorkshire Ripper.' Dodd Pollen waved slender fingers in front of his friend's face. 'Made you jump, though.'

Gordon 'Dodd' Pollen was almost the same age and had the same first name as his frightened companion, but there the similarity ended. Gordon Berlin was a small boy, introverted and painfully shy. Deep down he believed he was clever and funny, but he was too timid to open his mouth long enough for anyone else to find that out. Dodd Pollen, on the other hand, was an outspoken, self-confessed troublemaker. While Gordon wore a sensibly warm parka and shapeless brown cords, Dodd had on a black leather jacket, black jeans, and engineer boots. Gordon was a boy who lost himself in a world of books and was too awkward to talk to girls. Dodd Pollen liked punk rock and whistled at every passing skirt.

'What took you so long? I've been here half an hour.'

'Had a bit of a barney with my dad.'

'Again?'

Dodd's father was a Church of Scotland minister. He didn't like his son's clothes or his taste in music or, it seemed, anything else about his rebellious offspring.

'Yeah, but I got him back good this time.'

'What did you do, Dodd?'

'I broke into his church.' The teenager pulled a wad of pound notes from his pocket. 'He keeps all the collection money in his office.'

'Are you totally mental?'

'I did get a wee bit carried away.' The teenager clenched his jaw. 'Might have spray painted some graffiti on the walls while I was at it.'

'Holy mother of God!' Gordon gasped, acutely aware

this might not be the most appropriate phrase to use. 'Do you know how much trouble you're going to be in?'

'Tell me about it.' Dodd shook his head dejectedly. 'I don't know what to do. The police will be all over that place tomorrow and my dad's bound to point the finger at me.'

'Jeez. I keep hanging out with you and I'll end up in Borstal.'

'Not you, pal. You couldn't be more square if you were made of Lego.'

Gordon accepted the jibe. The two were the most unlikely friends. They had met a few months ago, on Magdalene Green. Gordon had been sitting alone on the swings reading and Dodd was perched alone on the roundabout, hands in his pockets, slowly revolving. Finally he had sauntered over.

'What you reading, pal?'

Gordon looked up. He didn't want to talk, but the boy standing in front of him had been too intimidating to ignore.

'It's called* The Great Gatsby.'

He had expected a smack in the teeth right there for being such a weed but the stranger just laughed.

'Is it?'

'Is it what?'

'Great.'

Gordon smiled timidly. 'It's all right.'

'I only read comic books myself. The Green Lantern *is my favourite. Hey, you like music? I used to like the* Rolling Stones *but then I heard a band called the* Sex Pistols. *They're ace.'*

And suddenly Gordon knew they had something in common.

They were both lonely.

The boy never told his parents about his new friend. They were protective to the point of paranoia and would never have let him hang out with such a rough type. And Dodd didn't tell his parents about Gordon. Dodd didn't tell his parents anything.

'Smoke?' Dodd held out a cigarette.

'I'm trying to quit by not ever starting.'

'You're such a nancy.' The boy lit a cigarette, tossed the match over his shoulder and patted his rucksack. 'I'm telling you, a fag would go just right with the bottle of wine I nicked from my dad's office.'

'What are we doing here anyway?' Gordon looked disdainfully around the dingy underbelly of the bridge. Broken bottles and crumpled cans glittered in the moonlight.

Dodd glanced upwards and winked. 'I got something to show you.'

'Are you crazy?' Gordon stopped in horror. The boys had climbed up a batch of scaffolding until they reached the barrier that flanked the railway lines. 'You want to go onto the tracks?'

It had taken all Dodd's powers of persuasion to get his friend this far. Gordon certainly wasn't about to go waltzing out onto the bridge itself.

'It's too dark for anyone on shore to see us,' Dodd coaxed. 'Where's your sense of adventure?'

'It's hiding behind my sense of not wanting to get killed.' Gordon hung miserably onto the scaffolding. 'Where exactly do you think you're going?'

'There's a gap in the barrier about a third of the way across and a platform sticking out over the water. I think workmen use it to get a clear view of the underside.'

'What happens if a train comes along when we're halfway there?'

Dodd pulled a tattered pamphlet from his pocket. 'This is the Dundee station timetable. There isn't a train due for another half an hour. We can easy make it.'

'I am not going out on the bridge,' Gordon said vehemently.

His friend's face darkened.

'Are you going to spend your whole bloody life playing it safe?'

'If it means I have a life to play safe with, yes,' Gordon retorted. 'Have you ever heard of a train in Scotland that ran on time?'

'I won't let anything happen to you. I promise.'

'I'm not going on the bridge.'

Dodd sat down on the scaffolding with his arms crossed. He stuck out his chin, mouth set in a grim line, as he always did when he was determined to have his own way.

'What was it you wanted to show me anyway?' Gordon tried to get his friend talking.

'Doesn't matter.'

'Are you just being crazy or was it something important?'

'Might have been.' The boy wouldn't look round. When Dodd Pollen got into a mood it could last for hours unless he was cajoled out of it right away. Gordon gave a loud groan.

'Come on. Let's find the damned platform. But then we're coming straight back.'

Five minutes later they crawled through a gap in the barrier and crouched on the little workman's platform that jutted out from the bridge. There was just enough room for the two of them, but Dodd was right. Any train crossing would whizz past a few inches away and never know they were there. The teenager opened the bottle of wine and took a large swig.

'Look at that.' He pointed east, where the Tay estuary widened out to the North Sea.

'It's the road bridge,' Gordon grunted. 'We could see it a lot better if we were on the shore.'

'Don't be smart, you tube.' Dodd pointed again. 'Look further out.'

Gordon squatted to get a better view. Through the supports of the road bridge he could just make out three structures hovering on the water like giant angular toads, each bedecked with a myriad little lights.

'What are they?'

'They're oil rigs.' Dodd pulled the cigarette packet from his pocket. 'They tow them south for repairs.' He lit a cigarette, his dark eyes reflecting the glow of the burning tip. 'That's what I'm going to do, pal.'

'Repair oil rigs?'

'Work on them.' The boy leaned back against the barrier and exhaled a stream of smoke. 'I'm fifteen in a few months, old enough to leave school. I'm going to go work on the rigs out on the North Sea.'

'You can't even swim.'

'I'll learn.' Dodd leaned his head on one fist. 'My whole life has been a struggle, like I'm drowning and I can't get to the surface. My dad is down on me all the time. Every time something bad happens the police come looking for me and I get the blame whether I done it or not.' His voice dripped with loathing. 'And this time I'm gonna get stitched up for sure.'

He gave a heartfelt sigh. Despite Dodd's bravado, Gordon could tell he was terrified of what was going to happen to him tomorrow.

'I want out of here, Gordo. Want to get far away from my stupid parents and the police. I'm going to go and work in the middle of nowhere, where I don't get any grief. It's good money too.' He gave his friend a punch on the knee. 'There's a boom on, pal. Oil companies are crying out for workers.'

'Don't hit me! You'll have me in the water!'

His friend just grinned, teeth white and even in the darkness.

'You could come too. We'd be a team.'

'I was intending to go to university and become a journalist or something. No offence.'

'Aye. Settle down. Get married. Have a kid.' Dodd chuckled. 'You'll soon get sick of that, Gordy-boy.'

'Yeah. If I was you.'

'Some day you'll wish you were.' Dodd looked at his watch. 'We better get back. Got ten minutes before the next train.'

The boys squeezed back onto the track and began walking towards the north end.

Halfway there they heard a whistle and saw a string of lights moving parallel to the shore in their direction. Gordon stopped.

'Where did you say you got that timetable?'

'Out of my house.' Dodd was staring doubtfully at the flickering lights. 'It's been lying around for ages.'

'The schedule changes every few weeks, you moron!' Gordon shouted.

'There's a train coming.'

Chapter 44

Gordon Berlin lay on the tracks, curled into a ball, Bobby crouching over him, shaking his shoulders. The man's eyelids flickered and he gave a low moan.

'I think he's coming round!' Bobby yanked harder and Gordon groaned again. 'Come on, Dad! Help me, Mary! Mary? What are you doing?'

The girl was standing up, looking over the barrier in the direction of Dundee. A long, brightly lit shape was moving along the shore towards them.

'Bobby,' she said quietly, nudging the boy with her foot. 'I can see a train.'

Bobby leapt up and looked where his friend was pointing.

'Oh, my God.'

'We've got to get your dad off the bridge!'

The children knelt beside Gordon. Bobby slid his arms round his father's chest and Mary grabbed his feet. They managed to carry him a few yards before the girl dropped him again.

'He's too heavy!' she yelped. 'We'll never make it.'

'Can we flag the train down? Will it see us?'

'It's too dark. The torches were in the rucksack I threw away!'

'I saw a little platform a few hundred yards back. It's big enough to climb out on.'

'That's too far to drag your dad!'

'I know.' Bobby grabbed Mary and pushed her away. 'You go and get on it. I'm going to stay here.'

'That's insane!'

'Every second you argue, I have less time!' Bobby shoved his friend harder. 'Please!'

'What if you can't wake him up?'

'I'll think of something! Just go!'

'I'm not leaving you!'

'Mary,' Bobby said quietly. 'Don't make me choose between saving you and saving my dad. Because I'll choose you and then I'll never be able to live with what I've done.' He clasped his hands together. 'Please have faith in *me*.'

Mary started to argue, but the look in Bobby's eyes stopped her.

Instead she leaned forward and kissed him on the lips.

'You better not die,' she whispered. 'Because I love you.'

And uttering that statement, more than anything else, made her turn and run.

Eddie Hall was seated on the prow of the *Lillian Gish*, the tin whistle stuck in his back pocket. Captain Morrison was peering through the wheelhouse window, using the crewman's hand signals to steer the ship up the river. They had already passed under the road bridge and were approaching the railway bridge. Eddie's heart was thundering. It seemed they might reach their destination after all.

He glanced up at the approaching iron structure and his face went white.

'Skipper! There's a kid on the bridge!'

He could just make her out. A girl standing on a tiny platform jutting out from the main body of the construction. She was waving frantically at them.

'Did you hear me? There's a girl on the bridge!'

'What the hell do you want *me* to do?' Captain Morrison stuck his head out of the wheelhouse.

'We have to rescue her!'

'The tidal wave must be right behind us. We'll be lucky to make it ourselves, never mind stopping to pick up a passenger.'

Eddie thought of his own daughter, safe in the hills of Aviemore.

'We can't just leave her!'

'You want to play the hero and lose your share of the money, be my guest.' The captain nodded in the direction of the ship's only lifeboat. 'Feel free to lower it and head for the girl.'

'And then what?'

'Then shout for her to damn well jump.'

Chapter 45

Dundee:
5 January 1977

A s the express clacked onto the bridge Gordon and
Dodd raced back towards the workman's platform.
There was a northbound track running parallel to the
one they were on, but the gap between the two sets of rails
led straight down to the water and it was too wide to jump.

'We're not going to make it!' the smaller boy shouted,
his voice clogged with terror.

'I know! Get onto the barrier!' Dodd swerved and
launched himself at the iron wall bordering the side of the
bridge. Gordon ran a few yards further, then did the same,
clambering up the side and onto the narrow rim.

The moment he climbed up he knew it would do no
good. The top of the barrier was already beginning to shake
with the vibrations of the approaching express. When the
train thundered past he would either be dragged under the
wheels by the slipstream or catapulted off the barrier and
down into the black water.

'We're going to be killed!'

'Hang over the side until the train goes past!'

'Are you nuts?'

'We don't have a choice!'

Weeping, the terrified boy lowered his legs over the river side of the rail where they dangled in empty air. There weren't any footholds on the smooth metal, not even exposed bolts or rivets. His entire weight rested on his elbows and forearms.

The express reached him. First the engine and then the carriages swept past, illuminated mayhem accompanied by a jackhammer din. The barrier was now vibrating violently and Gordon felt himself slipping. He wriggled his body frantically as he tried to keep his arms on top of the rail, digging his nails into the metal until they splintered and broke.

First his elbows then his forearms were jolted from their precarious hold and the boy sank a foot, hands instinctively grabbing the jutting lip of the barrier.

Then he was hanging in mid air. The last carriage of the express roared by, red tail-lights fading away, along with the pneumatic sound of wheels on tracks. Gordon tried to pull himself up, until his arms burned with the effort, but he simply didn't have the strength.

'Dodd!' he screamed. 'I'm going to fall!'

Silence.

'Dodd! Where are you!'

A pair of hands appeared above him on the edge of the parapet, then his friend hauled himself up and peered over the side.

'You had to pick the only bit of bloody barrier that hasn't got struts to stand on,' he shouted. 'You absolute wally!'

'Oh, God. I'm going to fall!' Gordon felt as if he would pass out. 'Please don't let me fall!'

Dodd put his hands round his friend's wrists and heaved. Gordon shot up a few inches and then slid back again.

'You're too heavy!'

'Don't let me die!'

'Hold on, you pain in the arse. I'm coming.' Dodd swivelled himself round on top of the barrier. Then he too lowered himself onto his elbows so that he dangled next to Gordon.

'Grab my belt.'

Gordon grasped hold of the boy's jacket and pulled himself up a few inches. It gave him enough extra height to get a leg round his friend's waist. He shifted his hand quickly from Dodd's jacket to his shoulder and pushed. The other arm slipped over the top of the barrier. He planted a foot on Dodd's back and thrust down.

'Ow!' his friend yelped. 'Go on a diet, will you?'

With a monumental effort Gordon hauled himself onto the barrier, rolling over and down the other side, landing heavily on the track. The impact knocked the breath from his body and he cried out in pain.

'Gordon.' Dodd's forlorn voice came from the other side of the metal wall. 'I think I'm stuck.'

The boy got to his feet and climbed the parapet again, his stomach churning.

Gordon's final push had dislodged Dodd Pollen's elbows and his friend was hanging from the barrier by his hands, exactly as he had been. Dodd's jaw went rigid with effort as he tried to pull himself up, but he no longer had the strength to do it. Gordon seized the boy's wrists and hauled. The positions were reversed, but the result was the same. Dodd was too heavy to drag to safety.

'I can't do it!'

'I'm slipping.' Dodd's voice, at last, betrayed his fear. 'You have to lower yourself a bit, like I did.'

'It won't work,' Gordon sobbed. 'I'm not strong enough. We'll both fall.'

'You got to try! You can do this, pal. You don't have to lower yourself right down, just a bit so I can get hold of you properly.'

'I can't. I hurt my arm when I fell!'

'That's not true!'

'I haven't got the strength!'

'You can't let me die, Gordy-boy.' Dodd's voice sounded helpless and small. 'I've got plans.'

Gordon grabbed his friend's wrists again, put his feet on the barrier and pulled until every muscle in his body was straining. He threw his head back and roared with pain and fear and self-loathing, staring wildly at the heavens, at the stars, at the struts of the bridge crisscrossing the moon. Anywhere but at his friend's face.

He pulled until Dodd Pollen's wrists slipped through his fingers.

There was a scream from the other side of the barrier. Gordon leapt forward, throwing his upper body onto the ledge, trying to grab Dodd's hands one last time.

Pain and abject horror were plainly visible on Dodd Pollen's face as he plunged downwards, heading for the black water. Then there was a small splash, a pitiful sound in the darkness.

Gordon sprinted back across the bridge and dashed down the embankment into Magdalene Green, looking for a telephone box to call the police. It was five minutes before he found one.

The handset was missing and the coin slot smashed and covered in graffiti.

The teenager slumped down beside it and wept.

He knew his best friend couldn't swim. He knew how cold the Tay must be in mid winter.

He knew that Dodd Pollen was gone.

Eventually Gordon's tears subsided. He got to his feet and glowered at the bridge, shoulders heaving with dry sobs. Then he walked home. His body stopped shaking. He stuck out his chin and set his mouth in a grim line.

His mother and father were in the living room, watching Coronation Street. Ignoring their warm hello, Gordon went to his bedroom and got out his photograph album. He sat with a red crayon and violently scored out every image of himself that had ever been taken.

Dodd Pollen's body floated out to sea, face down, on the estuary tide. Under the railway bridge it bobbed and past the oil rigs where he so badly wanted to work. Finally it sank beneath the waves, pulled down by the weight of sodden clothes.

It was never recovered.

Chapter 46

Bobby pounded his father's chest. The train was rounding the corner from the shoreline and moving onto the bridge.

'Please, Dad! Please, please wake up!' He got to his feet and waved frantically at the troop train. But the bridge was almost pitch black, the engine was travelling at breakneck speed and he knew, instinctively, that the driver wouldn't see them until it was too late. The bridge was beginning to rattle as the locomotive bore down on them.

'Bobby?'

The teenager spun round. His father was sitting up.

'Dad!'

'How the hell did I get here?'

Bobby pointed, his throat too dry to speak. His father looked round and saw the train. He blinked rapidly. Then his demeanour changed and he got to his feet.

'Get onto the barrier. Climb up and hang over the side.'

'What?'

'Just do it!'

He hurried his son to the edge of the bridge and they clambered onto the top of the parapet.

'Don't use your elbows to support yourself. The train's vibrations will just dislodge them.' Gordon lowered himself until he hung by his hands. 'Do what I do. If you feel yourself slipping, put your arms and legs around me and hold on.'

The last troop train from Dundee roared past. The barrier shook and rattled and Bobby felt his fingers being dislodged.

'Dad, I'm going to fall!'

'The whole damned bridge to choose from and I pick exactly the same spot as last time,' Gordon murmured in disgust.

He let go with one hand and grabbed his son round the waist with the other.

'You can't hold on with one arm, Dad!'

'I am NOT letting you die!' The muscles on Gordon's neck bulged and he clenched his jaw in determination.

One of Bobby's hands slipped from the rim and he gave a squeal of terror.

'Climb up my body,' his father commanded. 'Get back on the bridge!'

'I can't!'

'You can!'

'Dad.' Bobby choked back a sob. 'I hurt my shoulder when I bust open that shop door. I can't use my arm properly.'

His father's mouth trembled and he screwed his eyes shut.

'But *you* can climb back and pull me up, can't you?' his son pleaded.

'I can't, Bobby. I got no more energy.' Gordon looked into his son's eyes, his own glistening.

'Then let me drop. You can pull yourself up if you're not hanging on to me.'

Gordon Berlin kissed his son on the forehead.

'That I will not do. But, believe me, I am an *excellent* swimmer.'

And he let go.

With a double yell, Bobby and his father dropped down into the darkness and hit the freezing waters of the Tay.

The next minutes were a blur for Bobby Berlin. The impact of the fall almost knocked him out. His mouth filled with water and he sank into darkness until he thought his lungs were going to explode. Then he felt arms around his waist and a soaring sensation as he lost consciousness.

The next thing he knew he was lying on the hard wooden bench of what seemed to be a lifeboat. Mary and Gordon were bending over him, wet hair and huge grins plastered across their faces.

'Welcome aboard, Bobby.' Mary threw her arms round his neck and gave him a hug.

'I don't know what you're all so damned cheerful about!' A sandy-haired man with a large moustache popped up behind Gordon. 'I bet the tidal wave is only minutes away. We got to try and row for shore. Get onto the roof of a building.'

'What are you talking about? What tidal wave?'

'Where have you been the last two days?' the sailor cried. 'Down an effing mineshaft?'

Bobby and Mary glanced at each other.

'That's why the place is abandoned!' the boy spluttered.

'It's due to hit any minute.' Eddie Hall dug frantically under the seats and began pulling out a set of oars. Bobby's father grabbed him.

'Is this something to do with the Storegga region?'

'The whole sodding shelf has collapsed.' Eddie shook off Gordon's grip. 'How could you not know?'

Bobby's father threw himself towards the rail of the lifeboat and leaned over.

'The water's going down. That means the wave is just offshore. It's sucking the whole estuary out to sea. Then it's going to come piledriving back as a giant wall of water.'

'I thought you didn't know about the tidal wave?' Eddie returned to hauling out the oars.

'I didn't, but I know what it will do.' Gordon began looking under the seats. 'Forget about the oars, we'll never make it to shore and it wouldn't save us if we did. We need tarpaulin.'

He looked up. The children were staring at him in shock.

'Look for tarpaulin, dammit! We need to cover the top of the lifeboat and fasten it down.'

'You don't think you're Dodd Pollen any more,' Bobby said.

'How do you know about Dodd? I've never told anyone about him.'

'Oh God. I've picked up a bunch of lunatics!' Eddie moaned. 'I should have left you all in the water.'

'We lunatics are about to save your life.' Gordon dropped

to his knees and looked under the seats again. 'If we can cover the top of the boat and make it as watertight as possible, we might just ride out the wave. Lifeboats are made to withstand all sorts of conditions and they float like corks.'

'The tarp's under the bow.' Eddie gripped Bobby's father by the collar and pulled him in the right direction. 'Here.'

The two dragged out a bright yellow waterproof sheet, fringed with short pieces of rope.

'Spread it out over the stern and start fastening the ropes to those little hooks on the side,' Eddie instructed. 'Tie them tight as possible.'

'Work your way back from stern to prow,' Gordon added. 'Then we'll get below the tarp and fasten the last few ties from underneath.' He gave Eddie a puzzled look. 'What in God's name are you doing in the middle of the Tay in a lifeboat?'

'Came from that trawler.' Eddie pointed to the *Lillian Gish*, steaming west half a mile further down the river. 'My captain's still on it.'

'Too bad.' Gordon began fastening the ropes quickly and efficiently.

'He's a dead man.'

By the time the makeshift crew had fastened most of the tarpaulin, the level of the Tay had sunk to a few feet and the lifeboat had been sucked several hundred yards seaward. Vast expanses of the Fife and Tayside shoreline were exposed that hadn't felt the breath of the wind for thousands of years.

'Bobby and Mary. Get under one of the benches and wedge yourself in as tightly as possible. Hold on to each other. We're going to get thrown around a lot.'

'There's rope under the starboard bench,' Eddie broke in. 'C'mon. I'll try and tie you so you're more secure.'

Bobby, Mary, and the sailor vanished under the tarpaulin. Gordon stood up and took one last look at the railway bridge. He turned in time to see a massive curtain of water rising, dwarfing the oil rigs in the Tay estuary.

'Goodbye, Dodd,' he whispered.

Then he too ducked below the tarpaulin.

Chapter 47

The lifeboat was small but that was to the occupants' advantage. Mary and Bobby were able to cram themselves under the side bench so tightly that they couldn't have been prised loose with a crowbar. Even so, Eddie did his best to lash them in place while Gordon frantically tied the last corners of the tarpaulin from underneath.

The sailor pulled the flute from his back pocket and thrust it into Mary's shaking hand.

'You take this. With my luck the impact will probably shove it right up my—'

'It's on top of us, Eddie,' Gordon shouted. 'Wedge yourself somewhere!'

Mary turned her head into Bobby's chest. Eddie skidded under the gunwale and Bobby's father scurried over and slid in beside him.

'Sorry about this,' he said, throwing his arms around the sailor's chest and pulling him close. 'I'm sure it isn't how you intended to spend your last moments.'

The occupants felt a sickening, churning sensation as the lifeboat soared upwards. Higher and higher it rose, like a lift ascending at impossible speed.

Then all hell broke loose.

Ashley Gosh sat in a gaily striped deckchair, on the roof of his house—a bottle of wine open beside him. At last they both had time to breathe. Beside him, propped against the railing, was a surfboard.

The roof was flat, dotted with potted plants and surrounded by an iron railing. Someone once told him that retired captains liked to have the same feature built onto their homes, so they could pretend they were still on the prow of their ship.

Ashley couldn't see the sea, just the Forth estuary and, of course, the ethylene plant.

When he was younger Ashley had loved to surf. He and his mates travelled all over the country in search of the perfect wave. In the days when he still had mates. He'd actually fired a couple of them from the plant, he recalled shamefully.

Ashley had turned off the radio. He didn't want to hear the news. Instead, he sipped his wine and watched the horizon hoping, against all reason, that Gordon Berlin had been wrong.

Then came the rumbling sound.

Ashley Gosh put down his glass on the tarmac roof. The liquid inside began to ripple as the noise grew louder.

He stood up and took hold of his surfboard, flexing his muscles and shaking his hands, like he used to do before he went out on the tides. A silver line appeared on the horizon, growing thicker with every second, like interference on a television screen, obliterating the landscape.

Ashley watched the wall of water eating up the land, his head tilting further and further back as the giant foaming curtain raced towards him. He flopped back down in his deckchair, the surfboard clattering to the ground.

'Twenty years ago I'd have ridden that thing, not caused it.' He closed his eyes tightly and gripped the sides of the chair.

Then, once again, he no longer had time to breathe.

Captain Morrison stared in disbelief as the city of Dundee crumpled like paper under a gigantic torrent of water. Behind him, a solid green wall, the height of a tower block, surged up the Tay estuary, engulfing the railway bridge. He saw the ship's lifeboat vanish, sucked into the onrushing monster.

The wave reached the *Lillian Gish* and pulled the boat into its maw. He felt the ship fall apart around him and an enormous weight crushed the life from his body.

The tsunami made no sound, but the lifeboat creaked and groaned as it was spun over and over, flung from side to side. The occupants were swirled around on a nightmarish fairground ride. Mary began to scream and Bobby dug his fingers into her back, whimpering in terror. He could hear his father swearing at the top of his lungs. Eddie Hall was silent, mouthing the Lord's Prayer over and over. Water shot in thin spurts through gaps where the tarpaulin's ties anchored it to the rim of the lifeboat.

Bobby lost track of time. Eyes tightly shut he shook his head from side to side, trying not to throw up. There was a splintering noise near the stern.

They were all going to die.

WPC Arnold had the accelerator pressed to the floor. The car veered from side to side as it rocketed along the A91 and she fought for control with every turn in the road.

She glanced in the mirror. Baba Rana flopped around in the back, held in place by the seat belt. Through the rear window, the constable saw a broiling gargantuan wave rolling across the landscape.

'Come on!' she screamed, hunched over the steering wheel. The road began to wind into the Gauldry hills, but the tidal wave, though slowed by the camber of the land, was still travelling much faster than the car.

'Bugger this!'

WPC Arnold swung the steering wheel to the left. The vehicle shot off the road, ploughed through a wire fence and soared into a grassy field, landing with a jarring thud. In front of her, a gorse-covered hill rose steeply to a copse of trees. With the accelerator still flat on the floor she headed up the slope.

The car bounced and rattled up the incline, throwing great gobs of earth from its spinning wheels. The engine whined in protest and smoke began to billow from under the bonnet. The headlights exploded and a hubcap shot off and flew into the air.

Up and up, the Panda went. The engine's screech was now ear-piercing and sparks cascaded from the underside of the car.

Then it stalled.

The constable flung the door open, threw herself out and began to scramble uphill. Her heart hammered and all she could hear was the sound of her own laboured breathing as she clambered frantically up the steepest part of the incline.

All she could hear was her own breathing.

WPC Arnold turned round.

The tidal wave had run its course, spent by battering itself against the Gauldry hills. Fifty yards below it had slowed to a stop. Now a great black lake, dotted with debris, covered Fife.

Shaking all over, the constable made her way back to the car and found a torch. Descending to the water's edge, she shone the beam around.

There was an oblong white shape wedged against a dry stone dyke, abandoned by the slowly receding water. It looked like some kind of boat. WPC Arnold made her way over to it.

It *was* a boat. A lifeboat, the top covered in ragged yellow tarpaulin, puddles dotting its pitted surface.

She could hear a faint giggling from the interior.

The woman pulled back the ruined covering and shone the light inside.

'Are you people all right? Is anyone hurt?'

'Yeah. We hurt all over.' The voice coming from under the gunwale sounded deliriously happy. 'But we're alive!'

A burst of childish laughter exploded from under a bench on the other side.

'We're alive! We really are!'

'You can untie the kids now, Eddie.' The first voice spoke again. 'Tempted as I am to leave them like that. Never seen them so well behaved.'

WPC Arnold crinkled her brow.

'Is that . . . Gordon Berlin?'

'Eh? Is that you, Joanne?' Bobby's dad stuck his head out. 'What in God's name are *you* doing here?'

'It's me all right.' WPC Arnold turned the torch on herself, face beaming with delight.

'Now please step out of the lifeboat. You're illegally parked again.'

Chapter 48

Mary and Bobby stood side by side in the little cemetery next to Our Lady of the Sacred Heart in Puddledub. The interior of the church was still flood damaged but the stone building, set on the crest of a hill, had survived the tidal wave. The chimneys of the ethylene plant, however, had been swept away—the clear blue sky no longer sullied by its smoky pyres.

Mary was dressed in a black coat and carried shiny leather gloves in one hand. In the other, she held the flute Eddie Hall had given her. Her grandmother's red ribbon, threaded through her corn-coloured hair, was the only splash of colour she allowed herself.

It was two weeks since the Storegga tsunami, and Baba Rana's funeral was finally taking place. There had been too much chaos in the aftermath of the disaster to observe normal protocol. Everyone was busy trying to house and feed a huge proportion of Scotland's population. There were too many people hunting for missing relatives. Too many bodies to bury.

Because of the damage inside the church, the ceremony was held outside—not that it was much of a service. The priest spouted a few platitudes about what a good woman Rana had been but Mary barely listened. He hadn't even known her gran. After the coffin was lowered into the ground the man muttered some hasty condolences, fastened his coat and hurried off.

Mary hooked her arm through Bobby's and looked around. Gordon Berlin was still by the grave, talking quietly to WPC Arnold. She was dressed in a full length leather coat, her blonde hair pulled back in a ponytail. Pinned to her lapel was a small medal. Gordon looked smitten.

Eddie Hall was here too, holding his daughter's hand.

Only six people at my grandmother's funeral, the girl thought. *And half of them hadn't even known her.*

She couldn't bring herself to dwell on that.

'How are you getting on with your dad?' she asked Bobby.

The two of them hadn't had much chance to talk in the last fortnight. Bobby was living with his mother's relatives while Gordon helped the police in their investigation of Secron Oil. Mary was staying with an old friend of her father's until the authorities found somewhere permanent to put her.

She couldn't bear to think about that either.

'Not too bad, I suppose.' Bobby glanced over at his father. 'He doesn't remember being Dodd Pollen. It's a shame in a way. I think that weekend we were as close to each other as we're ever going to get.'

Mary gave his arm a squeeze.

'He's trying though,' Bobby said hopefully. 'I think he's changed a bit.'

'I think we all have.'

'Mary,' Bobby said shyly, 'why don't I ask my dad if you can come and live with us? If you want to, that is.'

'I would love to. And I'll never forget that you asked.' She patted the boy's shoulder. 'But if your dad picks up another kid at a funeral he'll probably have a permanent breakdown.'

They both stared out over the hills of Fife, neither wanting to mention the reason they were here.

'It's strange, but I feel sort of empty now.' Bobby scuffed at the waterlogged grass with his feet. 'The weekend of the flood, I felt I was really doing something. I felt more, I saw more. It's hard to explain.' He sniffed and shrugged his shoulders. 'I *lived* more.'

'Me too, though I can't say I enjoyed it at the time.' She smiled across at WPC Arnold. 'Same with my gran, apparently.'

Bobby nodded and hung his head.

'There are so many people in this world who don't fully live their lives.' Mary glanced across at Bobby's father, standing with his hands stuck in his pockets. 'All of them waiting for a train that never comes.'

She put on her gloves and pulled them tight.

'I've decided I want to see a bit of the world. When I leave school I'm going to get a job that lets me travel.' She gave the boy a nudge. 'What about you?'

'College, I suppose. I don't really know.' A haunted expression slid across Bobby's face. 'I don't know *what* I'll do without you around.'

'Then, one day, you'll have to come and find me.'

Mary walked over to her grandmother's open grave, pulled the whistle from inside her coat and held it out over the freshly dug hole.

Gordon shot her a quizzical look.

'It's an old Romany custom.' The girl answered his unspoken question. 'You put something in the grave you think might be important to the departed.' She glanced down at the flute. 'This is the only possession I have.'

'Put in your hair ribbon,' Gordon suggested. 'It belonged to Rana anyhow and that flute's been through hell and high water to get to you.'

'Literally,' Mary agreed.

'Yeah. Seems a shame to part with it.'

'Not the ribbon.' WPC Arnold laid a hand purposefully on Mary's arm. 'You were right the first time. Put in the flute.'

The girl hesitated. Then she dropped the whistle into the dark hole and retreated from the grave.

'What difference does it make?' Gordon whispered to his companion.

'Did I ever tell you about the biggest bust I was ever part of? We caught a boat smuggling diamonds into the country a couple of years back.' WPC Arnold gave the man a sly smile. 'Being a woman, I spent a long time admiring the contraband.'

'I don't follow.'

'Long enough to know those aren't glass beads decorating Mary's ribbon.' The woman's eyes sparkled. 'The Nazis weren't after the *flute*.'

Gordon's mouth dropped open.

'Excuse me!' Eddie Hall said loudly. They turned to see him heading purposefully towards the graveyard gate, his daughter in tow. 'Sorry, but there's a funeral going on here.'

A small group of men and women had appeared by the cemetery wall. They were an oddly dressed bunch—the females all in red skirts and the men sporting red or white armbands. One or two were wearing hats with white bands round them.

A broad-shouldered man with a short black beard stepped through the gate.

'My apologies.' He turned towards the grave and crossed himself. 'This is the funeral for Rana Szeresewska?'

Gordon and WPC Arnold hurried over and joined Eddie.

'I'm sorry. Did you know her?' Bobby's father asked.

The man shook his head regretfully. WPC Arnold moved Gordon gently out of the way and held out her hand.

'I'm Joanne Arnold. I was the one who contacted you.'

Gordon looked puzzled.

'That is the girl?' The bearded man shook hands with the constable and nodded towards Mary.

'That's her.'

He left the group, strode towards Mary and bowed curtly when he reached her. He looked up at the girl from under long dark lashes.

'My name is Petsha Andree,' he said. His voice had a European lilt. 'Your grandmother and my grandmother were cousins.'

He put his hand solemnly on his heart.

'My family did not know Rana was alive. They thought she died as a child. During the war.'

Mary glanced across at WPC Arnold, her mouth open.

'I did some checking,' the woman said. 'Didn't think it was right for a proper Gypsy to go this way.'

'I formally ask you,' Petsha Andree straightened up proudly, 'may we Romany pay our last respects?'

Mary nodded, too astounded to speak.

The bearded man turned to the group waiting at the church gate. There seemed to be twice as many now. He beckoned to them and they slowly entered. Their heads were lowered and many cried softly as they began to file past the grave. As each mourner reached the hole in the ground, they threw in a coin or a small trinket. Some scooped up handfuls of dirt and let the earth trickle through their fingers and into the grave.

And still more Romany came. Cars drew up outside the graveyard and men and women began to get out. Over the brow of the hill two painted caravans appeared, drawn by horses.

'We waited,' Petsha Andree said. 'We did not want to intrude without your permission.'

Mary covered her hand with her mouth.

The line of mourners now stretched from the grave through the gate and out of sight down the hill. Eddie Hall and his daughter were looking on in amazement. Gordon put his arm round WPC Arnold's shoulders and kissed the top of her head.

Bobby came up behind his friend and squeezed her shoulder.

'I think *your* train is here.'

Mary reached up and held onto his hand, watching the great line of Romany who had come to honour her grandmother. Through a mist of tears she glimpsed a movement near the wall.

There were two Gypsy children flitting through the broken and twisted trees behind the graveyard—a boy and a girl—heading towards where the ethylene plant once stood. The boy was slight and dark and the girl wore a red ribbon in her straw-coloured hair.

Mary glanced round at Bobby, but he was still watching the procession of Gypsies. She smiled fondly at him.

They had chased each other through these woods so many times . . .

From the back, the children looked just like them.

Afterword

A trawler found at the bottom of the North Sea may have been sunk by a
massive and very sudden release of methane gas, scientists speculated.

BBC.co.uk, 29 NOVEMBER 2000

GIGANTIC TIDAL WAVE COULD KILL OFF NORTH-EAST COAST OF ENGLAND AND SCOTLAND

A gigantic tidal wave, triggered by North Sea gas drilling, could wash the
region away, scientists fear. A natural disaster, known as a mega-tsunami,
wiped out most of the North-East 7,000 years ago and experts fear
another could happen.

The claims could delay development of one of the North Sea's largest
gas fields. Top British scientists are investigating the risks of sinking gas
wells in an area of the North Sea which once triggered a massive wave
which flooded 250 miles of our coast. Some experts say if gas firms get
exploration wrong another wave could wipe out the entire North-East,
killing millions.

EVENING CHRONICLE, 30 APRIL 2003

Preliminary estimates show that Ormen Lange is the second-largest gas
discovery on the Norwegian shelf. The discovery well 6305/5–1 was
drilled in 1997 and production is most likely to start in 2006.

Offshore-technology.com
(THE WEBSITE FOR THE OFFSHORE OIL AND GAS INDUSTRY)

Jan-Andrew Henderson is the author of several historical and supernatural books—including *The Town Below the Ground*, *The Emperor's New Kilt*, *The Ghost That Haunted Itself*, and *City of the Dead*. He has also written two fantasy novels for children—*Secret City* and *Hunting Charlie Wilson*.

He lives in Edinburgh where he runs a ghost tour company, which requires him to wear black all the time and look moody.

Crash is his second novel for older readers and his fourth for Oxford University Press. His last novel, *Bunker 10*, was shortlisted for the Waterstone's Children's Book Prize, the Angus Book Prize, and the South Lanarkshire Book Award.

For more information see www.janandrewhenderson.com.

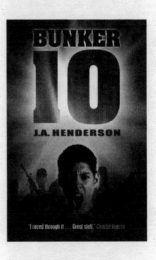